"We do seem to play off one another, don't we? I haven't forgotten." It was a smoky warning that made her want to wriggle closer.

She pushed her palm against the weight of the blanket where his chest was radiating warmth into her side, resisting him as much as reminding herself that she ought to.

"Don't pretend your reaction has anything to do with me."

"See, that makes me think *you've* forgotten how good we are together."

He hadn't moved, and she was suddenly fixated on how close he was, willing him to close the distance between his mouth and hers.

She should have said something pithy but wound up saying, "Perhaps I have."

And slowly, very, very slowly, the shadow of his shoulders shifted. His head lowered. The tip of his nose brushed hers and the heat of his lips settled feathery soft across hers. She let her mouth open slightly while he ever so gently deepened the contact, searching out the fit before he sealed them in a deep kiss and plunged them into a molten sea of passion.

Canadian **Dani Collins** knew in high school that she wanted to write romance for a living. Twenty-five years later, after marrying her high school sweetheart, having two kids with him, working at several generic office jobs and submitting countless manuscripts, she got The Call. Her first Harlequin novel won the Reviewers' Choice Award for Best First in Series from *RT Book Reviews*. She now works in her own office, writing romance.

Books by Dani Collins

Harlequin Presents

Untouched Until Her Ultra-Rich Husband
Cinderella's Royal Seduction
A Hidden Heir to Redeem Him
Confessions of an Italian Marriage
Innocent in the Sheikh's Palace

Once Upon a Temptation

Beauty and Her One-Night Baby

One Night With Consequences

Innocent's Nine-Month Scandal
Bound by Their Nine-Month Scandal

Secret Heirs of Billionaires

The Maid's Spanish Secret

Visit the Author Profile page
at Harlequin.com for more titles.

Dani Collins

—

WHAT THE GREEK'S WIFE NEEDS

HARLEQUIN®
PRESENTS®

Recycling programs
for this product may
not exist in your area.

ISBN-13: 978-1-335-40375-9

What the Greek's Wife Needs

Copyright © 2020 by Dani Collins

All rights reserved. No part of this book may be used or reproduced in
any manner whatsoever without written permission except in the case of
brief quotations embodied in critical articles and reviews.

This is a work of fiction. Names, characters, places and incidents
are either the product of the author's imagination or are used fictitiously.
Any resemblance to actual persons, living or dead, businesses,
companies, events or locales is entirely coincidental.

This edition published by arrangement with Harlequin Books S.A.

For questions and comments about the quality of this book,
please contact us at CustomerService@Harlequin.com.

Harlequin Enterprises ULC
22 Adelaide St. West, 40th Floor
Toronto, Ontario M5H 4E3, Canada
www.Harlequin.com

Printed in U.S.A.

WHAT THE GREEK'S WIFE NEEDS

This book was written in early 2020 as the social distancing measures began to take place. This is for you, dear reader. I wish we could all have a sexy tycoon sweep in to release us from being housebound and whisk us into a much more luxurious world. At least I can give you one for a few hours. Enjoy!

PROLOGUE

Five years ago

THIS WAS IT. Tanja Melha was a modern woman and she would go after what she wanted.

Which happened to be a man, leaving her to wonder exactly how modern she really was, but she was also human. Leon Petrakis was sexy and single, and she was headed back to university in a few weeks. This was her only shot at a summer fling that might cure her of a crush she couldn't seem to shake.

She sauntered down the ramp to the wharf, watching her step around the coiled ropes and other tripping hazards. The August evening was a few degrees cooler down here on the water, and laden with the scent of seaweed and tidal flats. *Home*, she thought, breathing it in.

Her childhood friends hadn't been able to leave the island fast enough, heading to Vancouver or Calgary or Toronto. Tanja went to the University of Victoria, and sometimes even that felt too far from Tofino, the small town on Vancouver Island's west coast where she'd grown up.

Which was another reason she had to *carpe* this man on this *diem*. Leon was Greek, but a citizen of the world, living off his sailboat. He was intending to stay the rest of the summer to help her brother expand her father's marina, but he was the type of rootless bachelor who could easily slip over the horizon at any moment.

As she came up to his slip, she saw him stowing something in the hold of the cockpit in the stern. He wore frayed denim cutoffs and nothing else but a tan.

Lord, he was perfectly made. She drank in his broad shoulders and the twist of his spine, the light layer of dark hair on his thighs, and the absent way he planted his feet and rode the movement of the boat when a rippling wave came in.

"Hey, sailor." It was supposed to be a casual greeting but came out throaty with the lust that was overtaking her.

He straightened and turned, unhurried and even more magnetically beautiful when his slow smile appeared.

"Hello, Books." She had a feeling he deliberately used her brother's nickname for her, trying to push her into the pigeonhole of "best friend's little sister." His black hair was long enough to show its natural curl, his eyes dark and brimming with masculine appreciation as he slid his gaze down her blue minidress with its spaghetti straps.

She did the same to him, noting the way the hair

on his chest flowed out from his sternum to dance like flames toward the brown discs of his nipples. Another darker line drew her eye from his navel to the brass button that barely held his shorts on his hips.

"I'm all paid up on my moorage fees. To what do I owe the pleasure?"

She dragged her eyes back to his knowing grin. He'd seen where her attention had strayed and liked it, which made butterflies take flight inside her.

"I wondered if you wanted company for happy hour?" She held up the bottle of wine she'd brought. It was a crisp, dry white coated in condensation from the short walk from her car.

After the briefest of pauses, he tilted his head and said, "How could I say no? Come aboard." He took the bottle in one hand and held out his other to assist her.

He didn't move back to give her room. When she stepped down into the cockpit beside him, they were toe to toe, practically mashed up against each other. He kept her hand in his and looked down his nose at her.

"I'm too old for you, you know."

"At twenty-nine? Please. I'm twenty-two. I didn't come here to lose my virginity." But she *had* come here for lovemaking. She couldn't pretend otherwise. Not when her breath was hitching so unevenly that her breasts grazed his muscled chest.

The corners of his mouth slowly curled. "Should I open this now or later?"

Oh, he was smooth. She told herself that was why he appealed to her. She wanted to know what it was like to be with a man who knew his way around every piece of coastline on a woman's body.

"Later." The word was a husk in the back of her throat. She couldn't peel her eyes off his mouth.

"Come below," he invited.

She ought to be nervous. In some ways she was. She didn't do random hookups. She'd had a few boyfriends and had dated since being at university, but her two relationships that had been serious enough for lovemaking had been hard cases of puppy love, intense enough to dent her heart when they fell apart. Sex with the first had been many frustrating experiments in figuring things out, the second a much more successful and satisfying pairing, but they ultimately wanted different things.

The bottom line was, she was hardly an expert in the arts of seduction and eroticism.

"This is nice," she said of the interior. It was tidier than she'd expected, given how devil-may-care his personality seemed. The windows were surprisingly big and bright, showcasing the gleam of the polished wood and stainless steel. The upholstery was maroon, the curtains smoky gray, the accent cushions sage green and rusty orange.

"Thanks." He stowed the wine in the refrigerator and rinsed his hands, then dried them on a tea towel, hip leaned beside the sink. "I keep it this way. I wasn't expecting company."

"Weren't you?" She dipped her chin in a small challenge. She'd been flirting unabashedly since returning in June. He had finally, this morning, given her a low whistle and said, "Lookin' good, Books."

Now he didn't bother pretending to be sheepish. "I'm a sucker for a miniskirt. What can I say?" His gaze went down to her low-heeled sandals. "And long legs. Freckles." His gaze struck the ones on her chest, then her face. "Red hair."

"Why didn't you say? I'd have been here sooner."

"You know why." He opened his feet, slouching a little lower as he invited her with a roll of his wrist to come closer.

"I don't," she assured him, trying to act blasé as she moved into the space he'd made. "We're consenting adults."

A fine tremble of anticipation accosted her, belying the maturity she was claiming to possess. Her hands hesitated when she felt the heat off his skin hit her palms, then she gently let them rest on the firm muscles of his upper chest.

His wide hands came to her waist. He didn't kiss her. He looked deeply into her eyes.

"Mixing business with pleasure gets messy. As you see, I prefer tidy."

"Your business is with my brother."

"Mmm." His mouth pursed as though he wasn't convinced. His fingers dug a little more intently into her hips, as though he was undergoing some small struggle within himself. "And you're here for pleasure?" His gaze was incinerating her mouth.

"Hope springs eternal," she teased in a breathy

voice, leaning a little closer. "So far it seems like you want to talk my ear off."

"That is not what I want to talk off you." He dipped his head, brushed her mouth once with his own as though testing whether she was sure, then he covered her lips in a long, unhurried kiss that sent an earth-quake through her, unhinging her knees.

She had sensed that things would be different with him. Stronger. More exciting. She hadn't known he would fill her with the energy of a thousand storms.

She curled her arms around his naked shoulders, holding on and moaning at how vital and strong he was, enclosing her in hard arms, crushing her breasts to his chest. The scent of salt air and sunscreen clung to his taut, smooth skin. His light stubble abraded her chin and the faint taste of coffee lingered on his tongue when he swept it into her mouth.

He was only kissing her, and this was already miles beyond anything she'd experienced. All of her was flowering open. She was kissing him back with an abandon that wasn't like her at all, and she couldn't help it. The more deeply he kissed her, the more turned-on she was and the more she wanted to turn him on.

He made a deeply sexy noise in his throat, and his fingers dug through her skirt into the crease of her butt. He squeezed the underside of her cheek, pull-ing her hips into contact with his rippled fly and the hard shape behind it. They were fully plastered to one another, kissing like their lives depended on it. She began to think hers might.

Leon broke away to whisper in Greek. It might have been a curse.

"I really didn't expect this," he said in his sensual accent, nipping at her jaw and chin before burying his mouth in her neck. "Are you sure?"

His heart was pounding so hard she felt it against her breast. When he lifted his head, there was something sharp and bright in his gaze. A warning? A revelation that he was as startled by this as she was?

Whatever it was, it caused her belly to tighten and her bones to melt and her hips to press forward into firmer contact with his.

His breath rushed out in a jagged noise. With a lithe twist, he straightened and angled her backward toward a door, gaze locked with hers.

She would have stumbled if he hadn't steadied her, narrowing his eyes when she licked her lips. *Oh*. Her abdominals contracted again. She hadn't realized she had such power over him. She did it again, more deliberately, and color rose in his cheeks. His jaw tightened and his nostrils flared.

As they entered the captain's quarters, he flicked the curtains closed. She dropped the straps off her shoulders and shimmied the minidress to the floor, leaving herself in the pale blue thong she'd put on in hopes he'd see it. Like it.

He bit the edge of his lip as he looked her over, one hand touching the ceiling when the boat took a sudden rise and dip. His other hand released his button and fly. He dropped his shorts and he was naked. Naked and aroused. Really, really… Wow.

She swallowed, her own hand going to the edge of the nearby shelf to steady herself.

He slid onto the wide mattress that covered the entire space between the two sides of the hull. "Join me."

She did, flowing onto berth and man in one motion, fusing her mouth to his as she did.

He was so hot! His whole body burned her wherever they touched. The steely hardness of him was almost hurtful to lie against, yet so erotically good.

His fingers trailed down her back, both possessive and light, exploring with laconic purpose, mapping from nape to shoulders, splaying wide and tracing her spine. Gathering into her sides and shifting her against him as though celebrating everything she was.

She braced her hands by his shoulders and continued to move on him in a full body caress, moaning into his mouth at how good he felt beneath her. Rough and satiny smooth, hot and hard, vital and strong. His fingers tangled in the strap of her thong and his palms branded her butt as he guided her to straddle him and move higher on his body.

"I want your nipples," he said in a guttural voice that nearly undid her.

She shifted higher, sat across his waist, hand braced in the recessed storage space over his head so her breast dangled over his open mouth. He began to suckle at her and her whole body tightened. He wasn't shy about palming her butt and stroking her thighs and sweeping his touch beneath the damp placket of her thong.

She'd been thinking of this all day. For weeks. Months. Of course, she was slippery and wet. She moaned and squirmed as he teased and caressed, sucking strongly and seeking the bundle of nerves that were so swollen and aching she nearly went out of her mind. Within moments, a sharp climax struck, turning her into a quivering, shaking, panting mess.

He released her nipple and looked up at her with stunned delight and such carnality she felt a fresh rush of heat into her loins.

"I want to feel that when I'm inside you." His graveled voice made her skin tighten.

"So do I." Her voice was nothing but faint breath.

They shifted and she kicked away her thong while he quickly applied a condom. He settled on his back and invited her to be on top again. To take him in.

He was thick and hot and so hard he barely felt real, but there was no denying he was all man. His hands moved restlessly on her thighs as she settled into place. His teeth clenched and his throat strained with his effort to stay in control.

"You've been wanting this, too," she accused.

"I have."

"Then why—?"

"We're here now." His voice was guttural, his hips rising beneath her. "Tell me if that's too much."

"No, it's so good," she gasped. She pressed her hands to the low ceiling above her and began to undulate on him, moaning freely at how exquisite it felt to ride him in the same rhythm as the soft rock of the boat.

He ran his hands up her front, caressing and stroking, thumbing her nipples and plumping her breasts and letting his hands come back to steady her hips as he began to thrust with more power.

She had never felt like this. Like she was pure woman. Like her body had been made for exactly this purpose. For him. They were the only two beings in this world and they weren't *of* this world. They were something exalted. A god and goddess creating the universe with the charged union of their bodies.

When his touch strayed inward and his thumb lazily circled her swollen bud, she groaned in the sheer luxury of letting the tension build even more strongly, one glorious layer at a time.

"You're so beautiful." His voice was both faint and distant, yet reverberated in her consciousness. "Tell me when."

"Never," she said throatily. "Let's stay like this for— Oh." A tiny shift in the tide, a slap of a wave against the hull, caused a twitch in their rhythm that sent a shock wave through her.

He made a similar noise, one of gratification and delight. Anticipation. He steadied her and said, "Soon, lovely. Hang on a little longer. When I say." His thumb circled and circled, becoming her whole world. The point on which she existed while her inner muscles squeezed him and he continued those lovely, lazy thrusts.

It wasn't long before the noise she made became tortured. This lovemaking was becoming more than she could bear. She couldn't find words to express how good she felt. Couldn't say or do anything but push her hands against the ceiling and hold herself still for his upward thrust. For his caress. Waiting and waiting for his dark command.

"Now."

They shattered into a million pieces.

CHAPTER ONE

Present day...

WHEN THE HARD pounding on the door sounded as Tanja
Melha was climbing into bed, her heart caved in. This
was it. They had come for her. She was a foreigner and
was being targeted for questioning. Perhaps worse.

Trembling, she dragged on her jeans. They nearly
fell off her hips, but tucking in her T-shirt helped.

Everything in her urged her to run, but where?
There was no way off Istuval, not since the tiny island off the coast of Tunisia had been taken over
by rebels. They were holding the island—and thus
her—hostage, all so some authoritarian in a far-off
country could have a toehold on the Mediterranean's
shipping lanes.

Tanja heard her friend and housemate, Kahina, call
out that she was coming. Kahina's brother, Aksil, entered and said crisply, "Kahina. There are men here
for Tanja."

Tanja's knees almost buckled, but she refused to
endanger Kahina when Kahina had been so kind, har-

boring her through all of this. She would face what-ever awaited her, but her hands were freezing and stiff, her whole body shaking.

Illi's little form felt snug and warm as Tanja touched her sleeping daughter. Her heart was sheared in two as she gave herself one last moment with her, biting her lip to prevent a scream of agony.

She didn't let herself give in to the hysteria. To think the what-ifs. There was no time. Heavy foot-steps were scuffling into the bungalow. She touched her lips to the cheek of the four-month-old and deeply inhaled her sweet scent. Tears scorched her eyes, and her throat was so tight she could hardly breathe.

As she straightened, she felt as if her chest was crushed beneath a slab of concrete. Her feet pushed through quicksand as she made herself walk out of the bedroom to meet her fate.

Four men stood inside the door. Aksil must have run from his home across the street when he saw the soldiers arrive on the stoop. He wasn't wearing shoes and his head was uncovered. He hugged Kahina pro-tectively into his side with a tense nod.

Two men wore olive-green uniforms and cradled automatic rifles in their arms.

The last man who appeared from behind them was as tall and wide and swarthy as the soldiers, but he wore a navy blue pullover atop black trousers and footwear that, in another life, she would have pegged as sailing shoes.

She brought her gaze back to his unshaven jaw, his ruffled dark hair and his fierce glower. The floor seemed to tip beneath her, causing her head to swim and her heart to swoop into her stomach. It soared, then hit the floor.

"Oh, my God!" She clapped her hand over her blasphemy—as if these mercenaries genuinely cared about religious observances. They imposed their restrictive laws for control, not true concern for modesty or faith.

But what on earth was her *husband* doing here? Could she even call Leon Petrakis that? They hadn't seen each other in five years. Not since he had abruptly left just days after their quiet wedding because his father had passed away without warning.

Do you want me to come with you?

No.

He had completely shut down from the charmingly seductive playboy she'd married. A week later, he had finally responded to one of her many texts asking when he would be coming back.

I'm not.

That had been that. He hadn't said much to her brother, Zachary, either. Leon had supposedly been waiting for the full release of his trust fund on his thirtieth birthday. He'd promised to inject capital into the marina when that happened, but he had ghosted the lot of them, destroying her brother's livelihood and their father's retirement in the process. Tanja had given up her school savings to help bail out Zach and still owed on the student loans she'd taken to finish her degree.

All of that meant she would rather kill and eat Leon Petrakis than be dragged out of bed to look at him, yet he opened his arms and spoke with what sounded like...tenderness?

"*Agape mou*. At last. I'm here to take you home."

He moved forward in long, confident strides, like the lion he was named for, snaring her with easy strength and pulling her into his tall, muscled frame.

Her heart lurched in alarm at the sheer size of him. She'd forgotten this dynamic energy of his, this magnetism and sex appeal. How he made her feel utterly cherished as he crushed her close.

It was a lie, of course. She felt his disingenuousness in the hardness of his muscles as he cradled her. She saw it in his features, distant and closed off. He wasn't so much older as altered. He was still beautiful, but now he was fierce. Hardened and serious. Everything about him was amplified. This was Leon two-point-O. Leaner and sharper and stronger.

The scent of salt breeze filled her nostrils along with damp cotton and faint notes of aftershave or some other manly, exclusive product. Underlying all of that was a scent that was masculine and familiar. Personal. *Him*. It was elemental power and a barbaric will that enveloped her the way his arms did, in a claim, like an animal leaving his scent on his mate.

Despite how false she knew this embrace to be, after so many weeks of worry, her body bought what he was selling. She gave an involuntary shudder and leaned into him, unconsciously latching onto him as a piece of her old life and the security and stability she yearned so badly to get back to.

She was losing her mind to fear, she realized, because some latent, ridiculous remnants of her crush on him pulsed heat through her. She hated him. She had decided that years ago, but instead of thrashing him with her fist and decrying him as the heartless profligate he was, she *relaxed*. Her most primitive self drew in his presence the way her lungs took in oxygen—as though it was something that could be absorbed and used to keep her alive.

Leon cupped her jaw to tilt her face up and stroked a thumb across her cheekbone. The men with guns disappeared, and tingles of pleasure raced across her skin as her husband bent his head and set his mouth warmly against her unsteady lips.

An unexpected spark leaped between them, bursting in her chest like fireworks, sending a singed line out to her fingertips, into her loins and down to her toes.

His flinty gaze flashed in surprise, as though he experienced something like it, as well.

They had only been lovers a few short weeks, but seeing that ember flare within him caused her own to intensify. Her mouth softened, and he deepened their kiss in a slow rock of his lips across hers.

She let her lashes flutter closed and leaned more completely into him. It was so intoxicating, so perfect and needed and right. She pressed into her toes, sealing their mouths. It was exactly as it had been five years ago. His kiss was hard and hot and held a hurricane of passion behind it that would have swept her into its eye if he hadn't tightened his hands on her and set her back on her flat feet.

She swayed, stunned to discover reality crowding in like dark shadows.

None of this made sense. Not his presence here or her pounding heart or the way her hands refused to unclench from his soft pullover.

Keeping his arm around her, he faced the soldiers, speaking French, which was more common than English here, after the local dialect.

"See? As I told you. She's my wife. She came to teach English, but when the changeover happened she was unable to leave without a male relative. I'll take her home now."

Changeover, she thought dimly. Such a well-scrubbed euphemism for *foreign military invasion.* She went with it, though. She slid her arm around his lower back and leaned into his side. Her other hand stayed on his chest, tensely crushing the soft knit as she gazed up at him, searching for clues as to how he'd known where to find her. Why had he come? She'd been sure he'd forgotten she existed.

The soldiers shifted restlessly, exchanging looks of deep skepticism. "You live here? Without any male relative?" one asked her.

Aksil quickly spoke up. "My sister and Ms. Melha—"

"Mrs. Petrakis," Leon inserted.

"Yes, of course." Aksil nodded. "Mrs. Petrakis

taught with my sister at the girls' school before it closed. I take my sister shopping when they need food, but Kahina will come stay with my family now." Aksil tightened his arm protectively around her.

Leon nodded as though it was all decided. He would have swept Tanja to the door, but she balked. The words *what about Illi?* formed on her tongue.

Even as his gaze flashed an urgent *don't test me* into hers, her daughter let out the beginning of a staccato cry, the irritable one that meant she wanted to sleep, but her tummy had decided she was hungry. Tanja suspected Illi was going through a growth spurt, and desperation was turning her inside out because they were so low on formula.

The sound of Illi's cry froze everyone into stillness.

Tanja looked to Kahina. Her friend would be welcomed at her brother's, but his house was already full of Kahina's nieces and nephews. Asking Kahina to take Illi would be more than an imposition. Illi would take food from the mouths of Aksil's children.

Illi might not have come from Tanja's body, but Tanja was her mother now. She wouldn't go anywhere without her daughter. That's how she had come to be trapped here.

There would be no taking back the way she played the next seconds, but there was only one way she *could* play it. This was her chance, her *one chance*, to take her baby home.

"Agape mou." She gazed imploringly up at Leon. "You must be so excited to meet your daughter."

As outrage flared in the depths of his eyes, Leon's expression hardened before cracking into a faint smile. "It's all I've thought about," he said in a distant voice.

"I'll get her." Kahina hurried into Tanja's bedroom.

Get in. Get out. Get a divorce. That had been Leon's straightforward plan when he had received the email from Tanja's brother, Zach.

Tanja is trapped on Istuval. She needs a male relative to take her out. My wife is due any day or I would go myself. Dad's on crutches and can't travel. Since you are technically still her husband...

Technically? He *was* her husband, despite the five years of estrangement. Dissolving his marriage hadn't been a priority while Leon had been rebuilding his father's empire. Divorce papers would have invited his wife to gouge him for a settlement, jeopardizing all he was trying to regain, so he'd let that task slide.

With this rescue, Leon had seen an opportunity to end things without her trying to soak him. He'd headed to Malta where he'd bought a racing trimaran, readied the vessel, set aside bribery cash in various currencies, and stocked up on diapers and formula.

Zach's email had said "they" were desperate for baby supplies. Leon had taken that to be a collective "they." That Zach was advising he bring infant goods to grease palms.

Leon hadn't been given a chance to mention the supplies or the money to his inquisitors. The moment he'd come near the harbor, he'd been boarded. He and the trimaran had been searched and the infant supplies moved onto the dock when he moored. He'd been roughed up, and accused of smuggling and trying to profiteer on the island's black market.

He had told the truth—he was here to collect his wife. He didn't have a marriage certificate on him, though, which had made the soldiers skeptical. The identification he did have could have got him detained for a ransom demand if they'd understood exactly who he was. He had a contingency plan in place for that, but thankfully it wasn't needed. Yet.

He'd been put in a vehicle and driven here to see his wife.

And his *baby*?

Given the supplies he'd brought, the existence of a baby was almost a blessing. *Almost*—because this was definitely not his baby appearing in the arms of the woman who lived with Tanja. He hadn't had any sort of contact with Tanja—intimate or otherwise— in five years.

"This is Illi." Tanja's voice was husky with deep, maternal love as she took the girl.

Something flickered in his mind's eye like a flashbulb taking a photo. He absorbed her tone and the tender way she cradled the baby so protectively. His memory took a snapshot to dwell on the fine details later because right now he had to stay anchored in the tension permeating the air around them.

The baby had neither Tanja's straight, red-gold hair, her pale complexion nor her hazel eyes. The infant's black curls and light brown skin could pass for mixed race if Tanja had slept with a man who looked like him, though. Which she must have done.

Why that dug such a deep thorn into him, Leon couldn't say. Their marriage had been a moment of temporary madness that he only recollected as a statement of fact. His father was dead. His age was thirty-five. His legal status was "married."

How Tanja had conducted her life these last years was none of his business.

But where *was* that other man? Surely he would be as affronted to have Leon named his baby's father as Leon was at having another man's baby passed off as his? Leon could hardly keep his dumbfounded fury off his face.

He manufactured a smile, though, hyperaware of the scrutiny they were under and that, regardless of who this baby's father was, the infant was completely helpless and innocent. If she was Tanja's, for the purposes of this rescue, she was his.

"She's beautiful." He tried to look smitten even though he'd never really looked at a baby before. This one was whimpering as she nuzzled her face into Tanja's chest.

"I'll make her a bottle." The other woman took the baby again and hurried away.

"I was upset that you and I were apart. My milk didn't come," Tanja said with an apologetic smile toward the soldiers for speaking of such things.

"See?" Leon leaped on her remark to prove his lie.

"Her brother told me diapers and formula were difficult to find here. I brought them for my daughter."

One of the soldiers accepted that with a bored look toward his compatriot. He seemed ready to leave. His fellow soldier wore the look of a man with a hard-on for power. Leon hated men like that. He'd been raised by one and feared he had turned into one, which was why he was so filled with bitter self-loathing.

"Why were you here and not with your husband when you had the baby?" the antagonistic one asked Tanja.

"Things are different in Canada," she began while Leon spoke at the same time. "My father died—"

Leon bit back a curse and set his arm around her again, squeezing in a signal to let him do the talking.

She was nothing but skin and bones. That alarmed him, but he was more concerned with getting through the next few minutes without an arrest.

"We married in Canada, but I had to return to Greece when my father died." Ancient history, but true. "Tanja was already scheduled to come to work here. She didn't know she was pregnant or she wouldn't have traveled." He gave her a stern frown. Naughty wife.

He felt her stiffen, but she smiled apologetically at the men. "By the time I realized, I was too far along to go back. It's been difficult to make arrangements to leave."

Flights had to be chartered and women weren't allowed to leave the house, let alone the country, without a male relative.

The soldiers flicked their attention between him and Tanja, seemingly aware they were being strung along but unsure what the truth really was.

"My sister is a widow," the man from across the street piped up. "She let Mrs. Petrakis and the baby stay here as an act of charity. My uncle is a cleric." He mentioned the man's name, and presumably the uncle outranked these foot soldiers because they both stood straighter. "He's aware of all of this. Let me fetch him. He will determine if all is in order with her departure. Then we'll have no more inquiries from their governments."

The bored one nudged the grumpy one and gave a coaxing nod. The other sighed and jerked his head to send the brother out into the night.

From behind them, the baby's fussing abruptly ceased. Tanja broke away to say, "Why don't you feed Illi while I pack?"

Leon was starting to think they had a Broadway act in their future, if not a career in espionage. "I'd love to."

The little midge was placed in the crook of his arm. Milk leaked from the corners of her greedy mouth as she pulled at the nipple on the bottle. Sleepy brown eyes blinked open briefly. Her damp lashes were ridiculously long, her gaze trusting and oblivious of the thick undercurrents threatening to swamp and drown all of them. She let her eyelids grow heavy enough to close again, the simple action causing something to shift uncomfortably in his chest. Like the door on a stone vault was set ajar and a whistling breeze was stealing in. It ought to have been cold and uncomfortable, but it was warm and beckoning.

From the bedroom, he heard the swift thump of drawers and zippers being opened and shut. If the women communicated, they did it silently enough that the only other sound was the gulping from the baby.

Leon didn't bother contemplating how outrageous it was that he was pretending to be this baby's father. All he cared about was getting off this island with Tanja. Zach could have warned him she had a kid, but fine. Package deal. Whatever. His help with the baby should encourage Tanja toward an amicable dissolution of their marriage.

Tanja reappeared with a small case and an overstuffed bag that she pushed an empty baby bottle into. "Is she finished? I'll make another so it's ready while we travel."

She draped a cloth on his shoulder and guided him to hold the infant there.

The baby wobbled her head, then burped and let her head drop into the hollow of his shoulder. She was the tiniest creature he'd ever held and provoked a strange fire of protectiveness that stung his arteries. Her little noises of distress had him rubbing her back, silently conveying that she was safe, even though they were all balanced on a knife's edge.

Tanja rattled around in the kitchen. One of the soldiers checked his watch.

The door opened and the brother returned. "My uncle is on his way," he assured them, sounding as though he'd been running. "Five minutes."

Five minutes stretched to a tension-filled ten, then an excruciating fifteen. At least the baby fell asleep. Tanja held her and gently swayed, her movement hypnotic enough they all watched.

She looked like she hadn't eaten in a month, Leon noted. Her cheeks were hollow, her mouth tense, her eyes bruised with sleeplessness.

That fragility made the pit of his stomach feel loaded with gravel. His memory of her was one of athletic leanness with firm, subtle curves. She'd been quick with smiles and banter, and had possessed a core of surety that had made him think their affair would be a simple pleasure between unfettered adults.

Discovering the incredible sensuality beneath her veneer of sunny confidence had been as unexpected as it was dangerous. He'd had a brief surge of craving for her particular brand of heat and had wound up blinded by lust into marrying her.

He'd since told himself he'd imagined that depth of passion, but her siren-like allure was still going strong. It was stinging his lips after a kiss that was supposed to have been a one-act play. He'd had to press her back out of self-preservation or he might have let it engulf them both.

He steered his mind from further exploring that pointless fantasy. A car was approaching. An engine cut and footsteps arrived on the stoop. The door opened and an older man with a white beard and a black robe and cap entered.

Words were exchanged in the local dialect. Tanja offered their marriage certificate.

Leon had a fleeting thought at how strange it was that she had the document on her, but nodded verification that it was his name.

Passports were produced. Leon's came from the pocket of one of the soldiers. He'd had to keep his cool when that jackass had taken it at the marina. Thankfully, once the cleric recorded details from both, he handed everything back to Leon.

The cleric asked Tanja a few other things in the local dialect, recording her answers on a form. Leon wasn't sure what that was about. An exit permit, perhaps. There were so many threads of strain in the room, he couldn't tell which ones were being pulled. Was there some irregularity in her answers? Her allies, the woman who owned this house and the brother from across the street, seemed to be holding their breath and standing very still. Leon had the sense they expected this entire house to cave in on all of them at any second.

The cleric handed Tanja a piece of paper. She smiled politely, but her lips trembled. There was a sheen in her eyes. Her friends were glowing behind their stoic goodbyes.

Leon didn't waste time trying to interpret it.

"Everything is in order?" he confirmed, forcing the soldiers to look at him. "I'll take my wife and daughter to my boat, then."

CHAPTER TWO

"I'LL DRIVE YOU to the marina in my uncle's car," Aksil offered as the soldiers left. "His plates are known. We won't be bothered."

Tanja had one last chance to hug Kahina, who had become like a sister to her, then her friend hurried across to her brother's house.

Tanja cradled Illi against her shoulder as she climbed into the back of the sedan. Her bags were so meager Leon didn't bother putting them in the trunk, only set the small knapsack on the floor and the diaper bag on the seat beside her before taking the front passenger seat.

Now she felt as though she was running, not even worrying over the lack of a car seat. It was a short drive, and her muscles were tense and twitching, her skin coated in clammy perspiration while her lungs felt as though they couldn't sip enough oxygen. Escape loomed so close she could taste it. She only had to make it a little farther.

Tanja didn't fully understand who Kahina's uncle was, only that Kahina had appealed to him when the school had been shut down and all the female students forced into seclusion. The cleric and his wife had interviewed Tanja about how Illi had come to be in her care. After a few weeks of making inquiries, they had concluded she was telling the truth. Illi's parents were dead. Her only living relative, her adolescent brother, was impossible to locate. The cleric had decided Tanja could continue to mother the girl so long as she didn't draw negative attention to Kahina or the rest of their family.

Tanja had inadvertently broken that deal this evening. She had waited in terror for the cleric to denounce her to the soldiers, but he'd calmly forged a birth certificate and handed her the document before accompanying Kahina across the street to await the return of his car.

"I presume I owe your uncle a donation?" Leon asked as Aksil turned toward the marina. Leon stripped off his pullover so he was only in a body-hugging T-shirt, shoulders straining the light fabric. He unzipped a hidden pocket of the pullover. "This is euros. I had dinars, but they took it as a 'moorage fee.'" He pronounced that with disdain. "I also have American dollars and pound sterling on the boat."

"You hope," Aksil said dourly, pointing to the glove box.

"Not my first unfriendly port." Leon left the euros in the compartment. "They won't find all my stashes."

"We'll see." Aksil dropped his uncle's name when they arrived at the marina and escorted them down to the slip.

Despite the security the armed guards had supposedly offered, the trimaran had been relieved of nearly everything that wasn't nailed down. Some of the goods were piled on the dock beside the craft.

"At least they left the sail," Leon muttered.

"Do you think they siphoned the fuel?" Tanja asked in an undertone.

"Less ballast if I have to paddle," he retorted grimly, stepping aboard with her bags. "That's cargo I brought so take what you need from it." He nodded at the packs of disposable diapers and shrink-filmed cases of formula stacked on the dock.

The soldier who'd been guarding the stockpile shifted warningly. He knew as well as she did how much formula was worth here.

Tanja took what she needed for a few days of travel and, under the watchful eye of the nearby soldier, gave Aksil a last goodbye with Illi.

"We're going to miss you both," he said, touching the sleeping baby's cheek. "My children will be upset they couldn't say goodbye. Siman will cry."

"I wish you could all come," she whispered. The craft was so small it would barely carry the three of them, let alone a family of six plus Kahina, but she meant it.

"We have protection here," Aksil said with quiet confidence. "And this is our home. You want to go back to yours. But you'll bring our Illi back to visit someday."

"I will," she swore. "Tell your uncle *thank you*." There weren't words for what he'd done for them.

If only he could work a similar miracle with Brahim. She didn't let herself grow emotional over Illi's brother, though; otherwise, she'd be tempted to stay, and Brahim had made her promise to take Illi to Canada if she had the chance. Hopefully, once she was safely home, Tanja would be able to contact him and help him, too.

"The map you wanted…" Leon emerged from below to hand off what was no doubt another handful of notes to Aksil. "And some chocolate for your children."

One or the other would be a final bribe to the mercenaries circling like sharks. Whatever got them out of the port without being shot at, Tanja supposed.

Leon helped her aboard with Illi, then tried the engine while Aksil cast off. The motor turned over and so did her heart.

She ought to be urging Leon to wait until first light to set sail, but she was anxious enough to get off Istuval that she was willing to take her chances in the open waters of a dark Mediterranean. Leon was a very experienced sailor. She knew that much about him, even if he was a stranger in other ways.

Her marriage had become something of an urban legend among her friends, only mentioned if someone was persistent about asking her on a date or setting her up. Since the summer she'd married Leon, Tanja's life had been school and work, school and work. She hadn't had time for socializing, never mind a serious relationship. Perhaps if she had met someone who had really tempted her, she might have felt compelled to seek a divorce sooner, but she never had.

Nevertheless, when she had come to Istuval, it had been with the intention of going to Greece afterward, to properly end things with Leon.

Everything had gone sideways shortly after her arrival. Had she procrastinated contacting him? Absolutely. She'd been so hurt and angry after his initial betrayal, she had resolved to force *him* to come to *her* if he wanted a divorce. It was a juvenile attitude she had come to regret when five years passed without a word, but the longer their silence went on, the harder it became to be the one to break it.

So she'd put off reaching out to him until she reached Istuval. Then she had told herself she'd contact him once she was settled in her flat and job. She had pushed that until she had her class schedule and her lessons started. As soon as she felt comfortable teaching, she would definitely let him know she was in the "neighborhood."

By then she'd been so caught up in Brahim and Illi's situation, chasing her absent husband for a divorce had ceased to be a priority.

Now here Leon was, arguably doing one of the most gallant, husbandly things a man could do. He had swooped in to rescue his wife *and* had shouldered responsibility for a child who wasn't his, without giving away the game.

Tears of gratitude arrived at the backs of her eyes like a battering ram. She could hardly see, but she braced her feet where she stood in the well of the outer deck, near where Leon took the wheel. With the baby clutched firmly to her chest, she waved at Aksil with her free hand.

Aksil waved once, but didn't linger. He exchanged something with the nearest soldier and made his way back to the car.

"PFDs were taken," Leon said tersely. "Go below so I don't have to worry about you falling overboard."

She didn't take offense at his abrupt order. She'd sailed with enough captains, her father and brother included, to know that even the best conditions required focus and potentially quick action. They weren't sailing into a storm, but it was dark and they would all be better off if she did as she was told and let him concentrate.

Even so, she was compelled to say, "Same." Turning any sailing vessel around to recover a man overboard was tricky. She didn't want to test whether she had the necessary skill. Not tonight. Not in the dark.

"Once we're under sail, I'll settle into the helm and won't leave it until daylight." He jerked his head to indicate he would be inside with her.

"Do you need help with the sails? I can put Illi down—"

"I can manage this alone. That's why I bought her. Go to bed." He might have glanced at her, but it was hard to tell in the dim glow of the running lights. "We'll fly once she gets going, but it'll be tomorrow afternoon before we reach Malta."

Was that where they were going? She probably

should have asked. "You don't have to stay up all night. I can spell you off."

"I've raced," he reminded. "Sailed sleep-deprived many times. Go. You look like you haven't slept in weeks."

"Thanks," she muttered. Had he met *any* new mothers? "Wake me if—"

"I will. But I won't have to."

She ducked her head to go through the small door, shuffled hunched over through the tiny space that was the helm with its captain's chair and low-profile view over the bow, then negotiated the short, steep ladder into the cabin below. The saloon was a sleek, narrow space with a galley on one side and a bench settee with a long, narrow dining table on the other. An oblong door at the end led to the only quarters and was taken up by the V-shaped berth with storage space beneath and a skylight hatch above.

Everything was minimal and modest, not at all the opulent sailboat Leon had been swanning around in when they had met and married.

He had lost his father's fortune, she had read shortly after he left her in Canada. That's why he'd failed to invest in the marina her brother had taken over from their father. Recently, Leon had seemed to be coming back on top again—not that she made a habit of stalking him online. On the contrary, she purposely *didn't* check up on him.

Maybe he had lost everything again while she'd been cut off from the world on Istuval. Typical corporate raider, successively gambling away people's livelihoods.

She shouldn't be so cynical when he'd just saved her and her daughter. She knew that, but she had resented him for a long time, and her exhausted brain was having trouble bringing the two versions of Leon Petrakis together, especially because she was also trying to figure out where to put Illi down for the night.

Cats and trimarans didn't list as severely as sailboats, but Illi still might be sent rolling. She had mastered flipping onto her tummy and often woke up that way. The mattress was firm enough she should be fine sleeping next to Tanja, especially if she was tucked close to the bow. Tanja felt safe leaving her there with a pillow as a bolster while she brushed her teeth.

She didn't bother changing into her pajamas, just positioned herself as a second wall of defense to keep Illi safely on the bed, realizing as she lay down that she was actually exhausted. Despite the late hour and her weariness—Leon was right, she hadn't been sleeping enough—her busy mind fluttered like a trapped bird.

Obviously, her brother had asked Leon to come and get her, but why had Leon relented? What would happen next? Should she bring up divorce herself before she left for Canada? Why did the word *divorce* cut like a knife through the center of her chest? It was something she wanted. Needed. She couldn't live in this holding pattern forever.

Then what? How would she pay for her flight home? She would have to tell him—

The engine cut.

Either they were out of fuel, which was so disheartening a thought that she bit back a whimper of anguish, or...

A sail snapped. The boat wobbled and Leon's feet sounded on the deck above her. She watched for him through the hatch but could see only stars. After a moment, the constellations quit joggling and began to move in a steady path.

It shouldn't have felt like such a relief to be steering into open water with wind their only propulsion. She had very limited supplies for her baby and suspected whatever groceries Leon had brought had been taken by the soldiers.

But when she heard him come inside and close the door, her entire being relaxed.

"Thank you, Leon," she whispered, and tumbled into heavy slumber.

Pink was staining the wispy clouds beyond the porthole when Illi began to whimper.

Tanja sat up, disoriented, murmuring, "I'm here, baby doll. Let's go find your bottle."

She had left the one she'd prepared in the tiny fridge, but when she went to the galley to retrieve it, she realized there was no microwave. Darn it, this might get loud.

"Everything okay?" Leon leaned down from the helm. He looked tired and scruffy, with a darker beard and weary circles around his eyes, but he was still sexy as hell.

Where the heck had *that* thought come from? The very last thing she wanted or needed was a recurrence of a case of the lusts.

She yanked her libido back under control and said, "She needs a bottle."

"Don't use the water in the tap unless you boil it first. I bought this from a fellow racer who had it stored on Malta. It's seaworthy, but the tanks are due for flushing. I didn't have time."

"Oh. Okay." She should have asked if the water was safe, but she'd been operating on autopilot last night when she had brushed her teeth. She had poured a glass of water, rinsed and spit, then drunk what remained in the glass out of habit. It had tasted stale and metallic, but she felt fine. Maybe a bit off, but that could be chronic hunger or mal de mer, likely both.

She only needed to warm Illi's bottle anyway so she set the filled kettle on the stove and started the flame. Then she swayed the unhappy Illi on her hip, keeping hold of a nearby ledge for balance.

"Soon, babykins. I promise."

Illi was sucking her fingers and pinching her arm, letting her know what a jerk she was for taking so long to give her the bottle she wanted.

"There's a hold they missed with emergency supplies." Leon directed her to lift the cushions on the saloon bench and open the narrow hatch beneath. "I had the chocolate in there with some extra bottles of water. I think there's a jar of instant coffee."

"And soup and porridge," she said as she exposed it and found the packets. It was all dry, hardly haute cuisine, but she was so thrilled she was giddy.

The kettle began to whistle. She found a coffee mug that would fit the bottle, then poured some of the hot water around it, lightly bouncing Illi while they waited for it to warm.

She made Leon a coffee in the meantime and passed it up to him. "I don't see any cream or sugar. I'd rather keep the formula for Illi."

"This is fine, thanks," he said drily.

She gave the bottle a shake and tried it on her wrist. It was tepid, but Illi greedily went after the nipple and drained the bottle in record time, eyelids growing heavy as she finished it.

They usually went back to bed after her early-morning bottle, but Tanja settled Illi on the berth with the pillow in place, then propped the door open so she could see and hear her. She came back to the galley to make a bowl of porridge that she took up to Leon.

"I can sit watch if you want to sleep," she offered.

He looked between her and the bowl and the coffee he'd set aside to cool, then to the various instruments. There was nothing in front of them except a light morning chop and a brightening sky.

"You're comfortable with all of this?"

"I couldn't navigate manually." She nodded at the rack of rolled paper charts, then clicked through the LCD screens on the hub mounted next to the wheel. "But it looks like we're a few degrees off the course you've plotted to avoid… That's a container ship?"

She clicked to the Automatic Identification System screen to see the vessel's ID and call sign. Another screen told her, "The depth is good, but I'll keep an eye on it." She clicked to the radar screen. "And I'll watch for that little guy off our port bow."

"And the radio?"

"Hold that button and bust into any channel with noise."

"Good enough." He slid off the bench, crowding her in the tiny space, head and shoulders hunched because the ceiling was so low.

She was slouched with a forearm braced on the back of his chair. All she would have to do was tilt her head and lean. Their mouths would fit perfectly. She knew that because that's how it had been last night when he'd appeared out of thin air like the Greek god of rescues. He had kissed her like he'd meant it. She had kissed him back like she'd missed him.

As his flickering gaze went from her mouth to her eyes and noted where her attention strayed, her pulse began to flutter.

Something flared behind his eyes before he set his jaw. "Give me twenty minutes, and I'll be primed for another twelve hours."

There was absolutely no reason she should hear that as bedroom talk, but she did. Which made her blush and shift out of his way in a small fluster, still clutching the bowl of porridge as she hitched herself into the pilot's seat.

He didn't bunk in with Illi, only went as far as the galley, where he settled on his back on the settee, knees bent because he was so tall. He crossed his arms and fell asleep in a blink.

She ate her cinnamon-flavored porridge slowly, wishing she could enjoy it more, but her stomach was really unsteady. Maybe it was the coffee. She hadn't had any in a while and it was pretty strong, but it was such a treat she refused to let the cup she'd made for Leon go to waste.

Maybe her tummy's protests were anxiety. Now that she was awake again, a tidal wave of apprehension was creeping up, threatening to drown her. Was there a Canadian consulate in Malta? She'd had three stopovers on her way to Istuval and doubted there were direct flights back. That meant she'd have to show a passport in Munich or Paris or some other country. Officials would want to be sure that Illi—who didn't look anything like her—was really hers.

Would her credit cards work? Tanja hadn't had internet access in ages and had failed to turn up for her first day of work at the accounting firm, even when they extended her job offer to accommodate her. Her last paycheck from her previous job had been twenty weeks ago and her sublet had only been confirmed for the three months she was supposed to be gone. That meant rent would have come out of what scarce savings she had left...

She sighed. Zach would scrape up what he could to get her home, but he wasn't flush with cash, given the new house and new wife and expected baby. Did she have a niece or nephew, she wondered? She would have to ask Leon if she could use his phone. Hers had been traded for food weeks ago. Which meant she would have to get a new phone and why did *that* feel like the most daunting task of all?

Then there was Leon. She glanced at his shins. How was he going to react when she asked for a divorce? When she realized what she'd done?

She had built him into such a sleazeball in her head. Too handsome. Smarmy. A horrible womanizer, a liar and an all-around reprehensible excuse for a human being.

Part of that had been defensive anger. She knew she was as much to blame for their rushed marriage. It hadn't felt like a hurry at the time, though. She had mooned after Leon for weeks as he came and went with Zach. Her brother had raced with Leon and had nothing but admiration for him, but when their father had decided to retire, Zach had come home to take over the marina. That's when Zach had cooked up a plan for Leon to invest in the expansion.

Leon had agreed to invest once he turned thirty and Zach had quickly been caught up in the excitement of purchasing more oceanfront property, chasing permits and rezoning bylaws, hiring engineers and architects. He'd borrowed heavily, expecting to pay it all down once Leon injected capital and the real work started.

Tanja had still been doing the books for the business. She'd tried to warn Zach against moving too fast, but she hadn't tried very hard. She'd been excited, too. In some ways more. Each time Leon came into the office, her entire being had sprung to life in the most mind-scattering way.

She had known it was only chemistry. Sexual attraction. Infatuation. She hadn't really known him as a person, but she had wanted to. When he finally flirted back, claiming to be too old for her even as he bent to kiss her, she had been over the moon.

Once they were intimate, her crush had bloomed into full-on enchantment. How could it not? Leon was gorgeous and led a glamorous life. For such an incredible man to look twice at her had been enormously flattering.

Then, a week into their affair, he'd proposed. *Of course* she had said a captivated and breathless yes. Their marrying would be perfect for *everyone*.

Given all the activity around the marina and Leon's travel schedule, they'd had a marriage commissioner come out on his yacht for an afternoon with just her father and brother in attendance. Leon hadn't wanted his parents to find out through online gossip so they'd kept the whole thing on the down low, tentatively planning a honeymoon in Greece to introduce her to them.

The honeymoon hadn't happened. Leon's father had died suddenly. Leon left and his promised investment money had never manifested. The marina her father had built had spiraled into bankruptcy. They had all felt duped.

Tanja hadn't wanted to admit she was married to the man who had ruined them. She'd gone back to school because she was enrolled, but she'd spent weeks hoping Leon would turn up and explain himself.

As the hurt of his abandonment solidified into anger, however, she had convinced herself that whatever she had felt for Leon had been for a man who didn't really exist. Had the sex even been as good as she remembered? Or was her memory of that as skewed as her vision of him had been?

Based on their kiss last night, he still had the same physical effect on her. She cringed inwardly at suffering that soaring euphoria and wanton hunger again. It was so superficial! Great sex did not equal "great guy," as he had brutally demonstrated.

Yet here he was, upending her view of him again, sailing into genuinely treacherous waters to extricate her and her daughter from a dangerous situation.

That didn't exactly put her in a position to disdain him when she, a woman who prided herself on doing things by the book, had pulled a fast one to get what she wanted. Which was her *baby*. She would make no apologies for fighting dirty to keep Illi fed and safe and *with her*, but still.

Perhaps he sensed the waves of conflict and culpability rolling off her. Tanja heard him awaken with a long, indrawn breath. His legs disappeared from her periphery. It had been more like an hour than the twenty minutes he'd asked for. She heard him clatter around the galley, setting the kettle to boil before he appeared beside her.

"Stay there," he said when she started to shift off

the captain's chair. "I'm going to adjust the sails. I'll clip on," he added in reassurance.

He clicked through the screens first, pausing to listen to a weather report in Italian, then went out on deck.

When he returned a few minutes later, the kettle was whistling. Tanja moved to make him porridge and coffee, then washed her bowl and sterilized Illi's bottle so it would be ready when she needed her next one.

She glanced in on Illi, who was fast asleep, then made herself a fresh cup of coffee and took it up to sit in the nook across from Leon where the sparkle off the water didn't blind her. No matter what happened from here on in, she had to say one thing.

"Thank you."

Tanja's voice was thick with such heartfelt gratitude it caused an itch in Leon's chest, one that made him think he should have known all along where his wife was, that she was in trouble. She shouldn't be sounding like he'd done her a huge favor when he'd only done what any decent man would do for his spouse.

Was he a decent man, though? The jury was definitely hung on that one.

He'd spent the night thinking about her, intensely aware of her in the berth below. His wife. A woman he'd married on impulse, mostly because her brother had learned they'd slept together. The expectation of Zach that Leon would propose had loomed like an aircraft carrier.

Which didn't explain why he had. Leon had never

been one to buckle to peer pressure, but he'd liked Zach. They'd been embarking on a business venture together. And Leon had been a different man then. He'd been blinded by lust and living in the moment. *Carefree*, some would have called him. *Oblivious to consequences* was another way to put it. He hadn't expected their marriage would last, but that hadn't phased him. At the time, he'd seen marriage as something that served many purposes so he'd leaped in without regard.

Tanja had been different then, too. Inexperienced more than immature, but brimming with vibrant youth and promise. She'd had plans for her life, not big ones, but solid, sensible ones. She was always in steady pursuit of them, too. Always in motion, talking and laughing and bustling, not given to sitting still as a wraith, wearing dark shadows beneath her eyes, her profile difficult to read.

Motherhood had changed her, he supposed.

"Zach didn't tell me you had a baby. Where's the father?" He flicked his gaze to the horizon, ensuring they still had a clear course.

"Dead."

Before he could mutter *I'm sorry*, she continued.

"I didn't have Illi. Not in the pregnancy and delivery sense."

"But you told the soldiers your milk hadn't come in."

"It didn't," she said wryly. "Because I was never pregnant."

"You adopted her?" The unexpectedness of that

news caused a bizarre shift inside him, like a see-saw that moved weight across his shoulders, lighter in some ways, heavier in others. It was disconcerting and left his ears ringing.

"Illi is the reason I didn't get on the flight when the other teachers were evacuated." She flicked him a glance. "I was fostering her. Zach put me in touch with officials in Canada to help with the adoption process, but internet was sketchy. Then I had to trade my phone for groceries and couldn't contact him at all. I warned him I would be off-grid, but I guess he panicked when he didn't hear from me and called in the reserves." She nodded to indicate Leon. "I should let him know you got me out."

"I only brought a burner phone and they took it. We'll have to wait until Malta. How did all of this come about? You being on Istuval?" Istuval was a popular destination for tourists, but usually travelers from Europe and Africa, not North America. Definitely not for anyone since the takeover.

"When I finished my degree and started—"

"You're an accountant?" He wasn't sure why that surprised him as much as the adoption. It was the career Tanja had been pursuing when she'd been at university. Once they married she had talked of putting off school to travel with him, though, leaving him with the impression she might have been after an MRS. degree instead of a real one.

"I'm unemployed at the moment, but yes. I'm a CPA. While I was articling, one of the firm's accountants returned from a stint on Istuval as part of a voluntourism program. It sounded interesting so I applied. I had to pay for my flight, but Kahina's school offered room and board for a nominal rate in exchange for tutoring women and girls in English. I also taught entrepreneurial skills. Basic accounting for small business, things like that. I signed up for twelve weeks, but it turned into six months."

"Is that how you met Illi's mother? She was a student?"

"I never met her. Both her parents are dead. I met her brother."

Leon let that roll around in his head. It just kept rolling, never coming to rest in a way that made sense.

"You're going to give me radiation burns, staring at me that hard." She sipped her coffee. "Brahim was fourteen. He showed up on my first day of class and said his mother was enrolled, but she was too sick to attend. He asked if I could give him a refund. I arranged it, but gave him some course material to give to her. He came back a few days later to ask me about it. He wanted to know how to start his own business so I invited him to join the class."

"That's shrewd business right there, getting his education for free."

"Don't be cynical. That's not how he was." She grew pensive. "Brahim is a very good person. He was trying so hard to support himself and his mother. His stepfather had recently died and he had a new baby sister. I presumed his mother was unable to work because of pregnancy and having a newborn, but she had refused cancer treatment because she was pregnant."

"Oh, hell." Leon winced.

"Yeah." She nodded and bit her lip. "That's how we lost Mom, so his situation hit me really hard. I wanted to do *anything* to help him. I offered to watch Illi if he needed to take his mother to treatment, things like that. His mother went back into the hospital and Brahim was staying with a neighbor, one who had other children including a baby. Brahim left Illi with her in the mornings so he could clean pools. That paid for the woman to watch and nurse Illi, but she couldn't keep it up. He washed dishes in the evening so he could buy formula, but he was so tired between that and looking after her, when he showed up for my class he fell asleep at his desk. I started taking Illi in the evenings and that turned into suggesting he sleep on my couch. We had a good little system for a few weeks."

"Why didn't you meet their mother?"

"I tried, but Brahim didn't want me to. He said the hospital thought Illi was with family. He was afraid if they knew he was relying on a foreigner, they would take her away from him. He loved Illi so much. I loved them both." She rubbed her breastbone. "When he told me his mother was terminal, I started looking into adopting them. It was going to be months of bureaucracy, but Kahina offered to extend my permit so I could stay and teach. It would have worked out eventually, but the café bombing happened. All the teachers packed up and left on any flight they could get. I couldn't leave Brahim and Illi. They were… I won't say they were *like* my kids. They *were* mine. In my heart, they're both mine."

She was pale as bone china. Her eyes glistened, and her voice was husky with an emotion that dug like nails into him. She was calm in her conviction, though, not trying to persuade him. These were the facts as she knew them. It was eerie, making his scalp prickle.

"Where's Brahim now?"

"I don't know." Her voice broke. She took a sip of coffee and her hand shook. "He disappeared a couple of times, came home with bruises. He didn't want to talk about it, then he got the news his mother had passed. He was devastated. She didn't even get a proper funeral because the military was cracking down. They closed the school. I kept thinking if I could just get them to Canada… But I couldn't even go shopping by myself. All the flights were canceled. Kahina took us in, but Brahim refused to come to her cottage. I realize now he was being pressured to enlist and was afraid to put us in their crosshairs because he knew they'd use us against him."

Leon swore and pinched the bridge of his nose. "He's a *soldier*?"

"The last time I texted with him, he begged me to take Illi to Canada. I said I wanted both of them to come, but he said he would be okay as long as he knew she was safe." Her breath hissed and she swiped at her cheek. "I saved those texts to my cloud account before I wiped my phone. As if anyone will give weight to a teenage boy's texts when deciding the custody of his little sister. I can't even prove she *was* his sister. Although they look alike. I have photos of him saved, too."

"How far have you gotten with the paperwork in Canada?"

"Not far enough," she said despairingly. "Kahina's uncle, the man who came last night? He and his wife pressured me to give Illi to an agency. Istuval is her home, I get that, but I couldn't—" Her voice broke again and she cleared her throat. "I kept asking him, 'Who will love her?' I really wanted an answer. Who would be her mother if her birth mother is dead? He tried to tell me she would be adopted, but we could hear gunshots the whole time we were talking. I finally said, 'If I have to stay on Istuval to be her mother, then I'll stay.' He said I could continue to care for her as long as I didn't draw attention to the family, so I never left the house."

"You've been under house arrest?"

"Only for the last two months, but most women are living that way. Kahina has a garden and a few chickens. We grow lettuce and tomatoes and peppers. It's been okay, but formula has been a killer to find. Lately I've been giving my share of our eggs to the mother down the street. She's been nursing Illi a few times a day so I could conserve what formula Kahina managed to beg, borrow or steal."

"That's why you look like you haven't eaten in weeks? Because you *haven't*? Bloody hell, Tanja. You need to eat, too." His alarm came out as fury, making her flinch.

"So does a woman nursing two babies," she fired back. She added in a mutter, "And that's how I knew I was Illi's mother for real. I didn't care what I had to do or whether I ever ate again so long as she wasn't going hungry."

He didn't know whether to commend or berate her. He only knew it made him furious to think of her withering away even as he respected her level of devotion. The frustration of being sidelined and helpless to go back and fix any of that put an edge in his voice when he asked with exasperation, "Why didn't Zach tell me all this?"

"I don't know if he believed I was serious about adopting them until I refused to leave before it was finalized." She heaved a sigh. "He's had other worries. His wife was having complications with her pregnancy. He wasn't in the mood to indulge what sounded like bleeding-heart antics on his sister's part. The truth is, once the rebels took over, I was afraid to tell him how bad it really was. I didn't know how much they were monitoring, and I didn't want to stress him out any more than he was. We were as safe as we could be at Kahina's."

"He still could have told me." Leon had to wonder if Zach had feared Leon would refuse to help if he knew there was a baby involved, but he didn't want to believe he'd fallen that far in his old friend's estimation. "You have the paperwork now, though? The cleric approved the adoption or whatever?"

"In a way." She swallowed and something about her imploring gaze filled his gut with gravel. "He, um, issued a birth certificate for Illi."

"That says what?" Premonition danced across his shoulders and down his spine.

You must be so excited to meet your daughter.

"Tanja." He could hardly speak through a throat that was closing like a noose. "Do not tell me you have implicated me in the human trafficking of an infant."

CHAPTER THREE

"THAT'S A HARSH way to put it," Tanja protested, but couldn't help a wince of conscience. "The cleric is a recognized authority on the island," she defended. "He's like a government official. He's also a man with very traditional views. He was fine with me fostering Illi, but he was only willing to release her to my care because my husband was there. It's not just about propriety. He genuinely wanted assurance that Illi would have both a father and a mother to provide for her."

Leon glared at her as he snatched up the radio and sent out a broadcast seeking anyone within hailing distance of Malta.

"What are you doing?" Tanja clapped her feet to the deck, adrenaline spiking through her, but there was nowhere to run.

"I can't dock in Malta, can I? I was going to put you on a plane to Canada, but what if we're questioned? No. I will be in my own country, with my lawyer present, when *we* inform the authorities that she's not biologically ours."

"I'm not giving her up, Leon!"

"I didn't say you had to," he growled back. "But I'm not going to play ignorant to a blatant fraud. What are you trying to do? Send me to jail?"

"No!"

He glanced away. Someone was responding on the radio. He requested they relay a message to the *Poseidon's Crown* to intercept the trimaran. He added their course and instructions that the crew stock up on supplies for a baby before they left port.

"What's the *Poseidon's Crown*?" she asked as he ended his transmission.

"My yacht. I'll be on deck. I need to cool off."

"Clip on," she said to his back, but he was already slamming the door on her.

That went well.

She hissed out a breath and gathered their few dishes, taking them to the galley to wash them. As she did, she heard the radio crackle.

"*Poseidon's Crown* is leaving port within the hour," the other party said.

She radioed to thank them and signed off, then poked her head outside long enough to inform Leon. He nodded curtly.

"What, no makeup sex?" she muttered to herself as she closed the door and went below again.

Okay, she had known he wouldn't be pleased, but desperate times.

She went into the cabin to look at her daughter. Illi was sleeping so angelically that Tanja crawled in beside her and dozed off. Illi woke her an hour later. She was in a ridiculously good mood, wriggling and smiling and cooing and kicking. She really was the most adorable child ever created.

Tanja played with her on the wide berth, telling her about their change in plans. "I know I said you would meet your cousin soon, but the captain has changed course. It might take a little longer to get home."

Her stomach cramped with fresh anxiety as she wondered how long they would be stuck in Greece. She shouldn't be upset about going there. Flights out of Athens would likely be more direct. She had been planning to go to Greece anyway, to beard the Leon in his den and demand a divorce.

That still needed to be done, she realized, experiencing a fresh, stabbing pain in her middle.

"I just want to take you home," she told Illi, nuzzling the baby and growing teary with homesickness.

When Illi began to chew her fingers, Tanja rose to make her a bottle and nearly lost her balance as she stood.

"Whoa," she muttered, quickly setting the baby safely on the mattress while her equilibrium caught up to her head. Her stomach rolled with a harder pitch than could be blamed on the boat, and a cold flush of nausea washed over her.

"No," she moaned softly as she realized she was sick. She touched Illi, but she had no sign of fever. Her growing fussiness sounded like hunger and a wet diaper.

Tanja changed her and used a wet wipe to wash her hands, remembering the water in the tanks might not be potable. Was that what was causing these knifing pains that kept accosting her? They were a lot worse than monthly cramps, something she hadn't had in a while, probably due to worry and weight loss.

She had to leave Illi crying while she clattered around the galley, using bottled water to make the formula. The small task pretty much wiped her out. When she had the bottle ready, she made a herculean effort and brought Illi up to the seat across from the helm to feed her.

The door abruptly slid open and Leon halted as he saw them.

"I have to look at the horizon," she said with a lip-curl of self-deprecation.

"Seasick?"

"Yeah." That's what she was telling herself, even though hot and cold chills were rolling over her.

"Eat something." He moved to flick through the screens.

Her stomach had writhed with agony at the scent of the formula. She swallowed back a reflexive gag and said, "No, thanks."

"Take the wheel while I make a cup of soup?"

It was all she could do to hold on to the baby and move those few steps to slide into the pilot's seat. She concentrated on measured breaths, willing the growing nausea to subside.

As Illi was finishing her bottle, Leon brought two cups of soup and offered her one.

Tanja averted her face.

"I know you don't feel hungry, but it'll help." It was an order.

"I drank some of the tap water," she admitted.

"Why? I told you not to."

"You didn't tell me soon enough. I did it last night."

He sighed with impatience and set both cups into nearby holders. His hand suddenly loomed in front of her eyes, startling her into recoiling, but he was only wrapping his wide hand across her forehead. After a moment, he shifted the backs of his fingers to her cheek, his touch cool and incredibly soothing.

His tone, however, as he swore under his breath was less comforting. "You have a fever."

"It's a water bug. At least it's not contagious."

"We hope," he muttered.

"Move then. I'll get away from you."

He stepped back and she wriggled from the helm, juggling baby and empty bottle.

Her struggle must have looked pretty bad because Leon locked his arms around both her and the baby. He plucked the empty bottle from her hold and eased her into the nook seat, scowling at her with a disgruntled expression.

"Are you in pain? Maybe it's something more serious. Appendicitis?"

"Oh, that's very calming, thanks. It's not that bad," she insisted, even though she was so weak Illi felt as heavy as a bag of cement in her arms, one that wriggled and kicked with joy.

It was so nice to see her full and happy, Tanja couldn't begrudge her energy. She played a game of wiggling Illi's soggy hand against her soggy mouth, saying nonsense things. Illi released her infectious baby chortle, making Tanja chuckle in turn.

When she heard Leon snort, she glanced at him and caught him watching them with the strangest expression on his face. Amusement, but something intensely personal.

He quickly snapped his attention to the horizon, showing her only his stoic profile, but her heart took a stumble over what she had glimpsed. Envy? Longing? Tenderness?

"Oh," she groaned as a sudden stab went into her stomach, sharp enough to push the noise out of her. She swallowed, but didn't think the porridge was going to stay down. "Can you—" She stood and shoved the baby at him before hurrying to the head.

A few minutes later, feeling scraped hollow, she shakily returned to the helm.

"There are anti-nausea pills in my shaving kit." He had Illi clasped in one bent arm against his chest.

"They knock me out and I have to look after Little Miss."

"I can hold her. Go lie down."

"If I'm lying down, I might as well have her beside me." She moved down the ladder and held out her hands.

He hesitated, then crouched to transfer the baby. "Call me if you need help. It's only a few hours until we intersect with *Poseidon's Crown*. You might feel better once we're not rocking so much."

"I'm sure I will," she said, but already knew it was a lie.

* * *

When Leon made visual contact with his yacht, he slipped down to tell Tanja. She and the baby were fast asleep. Illi wore a healthy glow beneath her light tan skin. Tanja wore a frown on her brow and hectic patches of red on her pale cheeks.

"Tanja?" He touched her arm and she flinched. "We're moving to my yacht soon."

"'Kay," she murmured, not opening her eyes.

He touched her forehead. She was dry and disturbingly hot. He swore under his breath. "You're burning up. Did you take anything?"

"Your kit is gone. Pirates took it." The mercenaries on Istuval, he assumed she meant.

He checked for it anyway, but she was right. "Hang in there."

"I'm fine. Is Illi okay?"

"Sleeping. No fever," he assured her after setting the backs of two fingers against the baby's soft cheek.

Within the hour, he was close enough to *Poseidon's Crown* that he dropped the sails and bobbed in the water. The yacht was manned by a crew of a dozen. One would sail the trimaran back to Malta, so there were two men in the tender that came across.

Leon transferred their bags, then woke Tanja. She sat up and shuddered with cold, hugging herself and trying to drag the blanket back over her.

"Wear this." He removed his pullover and helped her into it. "I'll carry the baby."

"I can do it."

"You want to drop her? No. You're sick." He took the baby.

Illi didn't want to be disturbed. She began to cry when he gathered her, but a fussy baby was the least of his worries. Tanja nearly hit the deck when she tried to stand.

"Stay there," he ordered, pressing her back onto the berth. He carried the baby out and handed her across to the crewman piloting the tender.

When he returned, Tanja had stumbled into the galley, clinging to whatever was in reach. She looked like death and sounded panicked. "Where is she?"

"Waiting for us," he said evenly. "Let me help you."

Her weight loss hit him as she leaned into him. She was reedy and light as he boosted her up to the deck and lifted her from the trimaran into the tender. She folded into a seat and held out weak arms for the baby.

Leon exchanged a few brief words with the sailor taking control of the trimaran, warning him supplies were low and the water was boggy. When he sat down next to Tanja, he wrapped his arms around her, both to warm her and to help her hold the baby.

She snuggled into him with a grateful noise, head heavy as she nestled it onto his shoulder. Then she picked it up to ask with weak outrage, "What the hell is *that*?"

"What?"

Her gaze went up and up and up as they neared the yacht. "That's *Poseidon's Crown*? It's a cruise ship."

"It has staterooms for twelve, not twelve hundred," he dismissed, keeping to himself that *Poseidon's Crown* had been touted as the world's first "gigayacht" when his father had ordered it.

"I *saved up* so I could go to Istuval on a *working* holiday," Tanja said with indignation, eyes glassy with fever and fury. "I picked Istuval because it was close enough to Greece to make the side trip affordable. I was *dreading* asking you for a divorce because I thought I might get stuck paying legal fees and I don't have extra money for lawyers. Once I had Illi and Brahim in my life, I didn't know how I would pay for a divorce *and* adoption. And all the while you have *this*?"

A chill descended. It might have been caused by entering the shadow of the yacht's seven decks. *Poseidon's Crown* loomed like a skyscraper above them. But it might have been that word *divorce*. It might have been every word she'd just thrown at him like sharp icicles that still managed to penetrate his skin rather than shatter on impact.

"My father bought it," Leon said flatly. "It was tied up on lease to a sultan for its first three years. I couldn't sell it without taking a bath. Keeping it has allowed me to borrow—"

"*I don't care!* You've been sitting on this kind of money for years while I traded my smart phone for baby formula. You're the worst, Leon. You are the absolute worst."

The behemoth with its stair-step decks of sleek angles and spaceship aerodynamics looked as though it was made of quicksilver and glass. It was modern and visually beautiful, and Tanja knew it to be indisputably luxurious even before she boarded.

As they approached the stern, a wall of the hull opened, allowing them to step straight from the tender into the yacht's fitness club. Across from where they entered, a glass-walled weight room held treadmills and ellipticals pointed to enjoy the view off the port side.

A purser greeted them, introducing himself as Kyle. He sounded Australian.

"Toy room?" Tanja asked, reading the sign on a door in the stern wall.

"Jet Skis and kite-surfing gear, that sort of thing," Kyle said. "Forward of the gym is our sauna and spa, but the specialists can come to you for massage or nails."

Growing up at the marina, Tanja had seen some swanky vessels. Beasts like this tended to anchor offshore, though. She'd never been on one to see the extravagance within.

"You have an elevator," she noted with a scathing glance at Leon as they entered it.

"We have four," Kyle said helpfully.

"Oh? How many helipads?" She was being facetious.

"Two." Kyle was serious.

"Two," she repeated with a curl of her lip.

Her air of superiority died a quick death when the elevator stopped and she completely lost her balance.

Leon caught both her and Illi with a glower, then took Illi and kept his arm around Tanja as they stepped out. He was so *warm*. It took all her concentration to make her legs work. She wanted to melt right into his heat and strength, close her eyes and let him take complete control.

"Have the medic come to my apartment immediately," Leon ordered. "Tell the captain to keep us in heli distance to Malta in case we need to evacuate her to a hospital."

"Yes, sir." Kyle quickly set aside her bags and moved to pick up a white telephone mounted near the elevator.

"Helicopters do come in handy," Leon said pithily as he steered her along what would be called a gallery in a mansion.

They skirted an atrium that looked down to the main saloon—accessed by a glass elevator, she noted as they passed. There was a dome of colored glass above them, and now they were moving through double doors into, well, it was nothing less than a mini penthouse.

On one side there was a galley fronted by a wet bar with stools. On the other side stood a business area with a stately desk, a monitor on an articulated arm and a printer on a bookshelf that held a handful of novels.

They moved into a spacious and bright area for lounging and dining. Walls of windows on either side opened to the wide, surrounding deck. The windows continued wrapping forward past a partition wall that held a fireplace.

On the other side of the wall was a walk-through closet and a spacious head before she reached the massive bedroom with an equally massive bed. It was situated so the sleeper could sit up and take in a one-eighty view across the bow or walk out to the private forward deck and slip into a hot tub.

Her weak legs folded and she sat down on the foot of the bed. How did one process this much wealth and attention to comfort?

Leon hung back in the main living area to instruct Kyle to leave the luggage and find something for Illi to sleep in.

When he finally showed up in the bedroom, she asked, "Why did you bring us to your stateroom?"

"You need help with the baby." He was still holding Illi, who was making raspberry noises against her wet wrist. She smiled and held out her arm to Tanja.

"I can manage," Tanja insisted, lifting heavy hands to take her daughter.

"Can you?" Leon scoffed, offering her the baby, but holding on to her.

Good thing. Tanja's arms felt like wet spaghetti. She couldn't take Illi's weight and wound up dropping her arms empty to her sides, whimpering even as she glared resentfully when Leon's brows lifted in superiority.

The last thing she wanted to do was rely on him, but it was painfully obvious she would have to. For now.

The medic arrived with a message from the captain. "We were hailed by the *Pennyloafer* on our way to meet you. Dr. Kyrkos issued an invitation to meet them in Malta."

Kyrkos was a racing buddy from Leon's school

days. He picked up the phone and told the captain, "Invite Kyrkos aboard if he's still in the area. Tell him it's a house call."

Leon then hovered, still holding the babbling baby, listening as the medic asked Tanja a few questions while taking her temperature.

"High, but not dangerously high," he pronounced. "My guess is that this will pass in a day or two, but I'd feel better if you had a doctor's opinion." He gave her something for fever and told her to rehydrate, promising as he left to order fruit juice spiked with electrolyte tablets.

"Can I shower while I wait for the juice?" Tanja asked.

"I don't know. Can you?" Leon made no effort to disguise his sarcasm.

"Ha-ha. Water was as precious as everything else at Kahina's. That's why I was in the habit of drinking whatever I'd poured." She grimaced. "And that's why I haven't showered in three days. Feeling grimy doesn't help me feel better at all."

"Go," he urged with a nod. "Don't lock the door. Call if you need help."

She sent him an *I'd rather die* stare over her shoulder.

He wanted to say something sharp about her taking advantage of the amenities on the yacht that so offended her, but he had a brief flash of how she'd almost collapsed on the trimaran. It had scared the hell out of him. She needed to conserve her strength, not pit what she had against him.

As for the vessel, he knew it was an obscene expense. He'd been considering unloading it, but it was damned convenient. It had brought him quickly and comfortably to Malta and was allowing him to take care of her and the baby with ease.

Her drink appeared as she emerged wearing his robe, still flushed and glassy-eyed, but with a healthier glow on her skin. He gave her a T-shirt to sleep in and she looked with worry at Illi, making no move to change.

He read the conflict in her. She was sick, but she still wanted to be the one to care for Illi. It was as clear as the maternal tenderness she kept showing the baby with such natural ease. It was a regard that was so foreign to him he couldn't help staring with fascination each time he noted it.

That's how I knew I was her mother, he heard her say again as he took in her sharp cheekbones and the way her collarbone stuck out. That evidence of deprivation stoked the frustrated helplessness in him again, the one that wanted to be angry with her for not looking after herself, but how could he fault her?

He couldn't. He could only order sternly, "Go to bed. I can hold her while I check emails. I'll let Zach know you're safe."

"Oh. Yes, please. Thank you," she said with subdued relief, and slipped back into the head to change.

Two hours later, Leon had watched a handful of videos on the basics of baby care. It turned out four-month-old babies didn't know how to sit up so he didn't need to be alarmed that Illi couldn't. For a few seconds, he'd been convinced he had broken her.

Which was all he needed on his conscience. *You're the worst, Leon.*

I know, he had wanted to shout. A weight greater than this tanker sat on him over some of his behavior in the past. Nothing criminally negligent, but not a lot that was particularly considerate of others. Then there were the things his father had done. At least he'd taken steps toward making reparation on those fronts.

Still, he'd been disturbed by Tanja's outburst over struggling financially. He hadn't sought a divorce because he'd been wary of what it would cost him, never dreaming she had thought he was so broke the legal fees would fall to her. Had she not seen a news report in the last few years? He'd been back on top for a while.

I traded my smart phone for baby formula.

That put a sick knot in his conscience. One that had him again thinking he should have made more of an effort to know where she was instead of trusting she'd moved on with her life and didn't miss him at all.

He realized the baby had fallen asleep in his arm. Her round face and dark lashes looked like an ad for life insurance or some other peace-of-mind product. Even his hardened heart lost some of its resistant tension as he gazed on her.

Don't get attached, he reminded himself, and gently set her in the cot Kyle had found, draping a light blanket over her.

He might have stood there and stared like a fool

for hours, but a muted bell pinged. He picked up the phone and learned the doctor was boarding.

"Leon. It's good to see you," Kyrkos said a moment later as Leon stepped from the elevator into the main saloon where Kyrkos was waiting. Kyrkos never missed a chance to catch up if they happened to cross paths in their travels on the Med, so it hadn't surprised Leon that he'd hailed the yacht when he'd seen it. "I don't think you've met my wife, Cameron."

Not this one, no. Leon had been at the wedding when Kyrkos married his first wife, and had only heard through the grapevine that this youthful socialite had elevated herself from office assistant to mistress and recently to trophy wife.

"I made Kiki bring me, even though your captain said it's a medical call. I'm dying to see this yacht I've heard so much about. Do you mind?" Cameron asked with an appealing tilt of her head.

"Not at all." Lavish crafts like this existed to be shown off. "I'll have a steward give you a tour." Leon signaled to the crewman behind the bar.

"I thought I'd find you bleeding out," Kyrkos said. "Who needs attention? One of the crew?"

"No—" It hit Leon that he didn't have an explanation for who Tanja was. She was tucked in his bed so he couldn't dismiss her as merely a guest. If Kyrkos decided she needed urgent care, Leon would want to be identified as her closest relative to authorize medical care so he couldn't call her anything but what she was.

"I need you to check on my wife. Tanja."

"You're married? Oh, my God! Is she pregnant?" Cameron asked with hand-clasping glee.

"What? No," Leon said firmly, reconsidering honesty as the best policy. "Can you show our guest every courtesy while I take the doctor up?" he said to the hovering steward.

"Of course, sir." The crewman drew Cameron away while Leon took Kyrkos up the elevator.

"Wife?"

"Kiki?" Leon countered.

"I know," Kyrkos muttered. "But now you're married, you'll soon learn it's better to pick your battles than lose the war. When did you marry? How was I not invited to the wedding?"

"It's a long story," Leon dismissed, leading him toward his stateroom. "We were headed to Greece, but if Tanja needs a hospital, we'll go back to Malta."

The good doctor came up short at the sight of the baby cot.

"She is *not* pregnant, is she? What the hell, Leon? You have a *baby*?" He peered at the sleeping Illi. "How am I the last to hear? Cammy follows every gossip site in existence."

"It's not something we've advertised. My main concern right now is Tanja. We're assuming it's a stomach bug from drinking some stale water. She's been running a fever since this morning and she's nauseous."

Tanja blinked in disorientation when he gently woke her, but predictably asked, "Where's Illi?"

"Napping." He pointed toward the adjacent room. "This is Dr. Kyrkos."

"Hi." Since she'd gone to bed with her hair damp, Tanja's red-gold hair was bent in odd directions. Her face was pale, and his T-shirt hung off her bony shoulder when she sat up.

She answered his questions about her general health and the onset of symptoms, said "ah," and accepted a thermometer under her tongue.

Her fever had come down thanks to the pills the medic had given her.

"I agree with the medic's assessment. This will likely work itself out within a few days. Keep your fluids up, your fever down. If things worsen, definitely visit a doctor in Athens. I can take a sample to the lab in Malta as a precaution if you like, to be sure it isn't anything more serious. We're headed there."

Tanja held out her arm for a blood draw and then took a cup into the head.

"Is she a model?" Kyrkos asked while Tanja was absent. "She's very thin. Iron supplements and a multivitamin would be a good idea."

Leon texted that instruction to the purser.

As Tanja came out of the head, Illi began to cry in the other room. Tanja would have gone to her, but Leon stopped her.

"I'll look after her. Go back to bed."

"She hasn't eaten since we've been aboard, has she?"

"No, but I had all her bottles sent down to the chef so everything could be sterilized and ready when she needs it. I can handle it." He was speaking with more bravado than genuine confidence, but Tanja looked so weak and peaked.

She wore an indecisive look, but Kyrkos said, "It's a good idea to give her formula while you're under the weather. Keep your strength up."

"Oh, um—"

Leon could tell she was about to explain she hadn't given birth to Illi and therefore wasn't nursing. He signaled behind Kyrkos's back to keep that detail to herself for now.

"Okay," she murmured with a small frown of confusion. "Thanks for the checkup." She went back to bed, and Leon waved Kyrkos to lead him from the room.

Leon gathered Illi on his way out the door. She was looking very pitiful with her crinkled chin and teardrops on her cheeks. She rubbed her face into his shoulder when he held her against his chest, digging her way further under his skin with the small gesture.

"I know you're hungry," he said, unconsciously echoing what he'd heard Tanja saying to her when she'd been waiting for Illi's bottle to warm on the trimaran. "We're going to get you something right away." He picked up the phone by the elevator and asked the chef to prepare a bottle, requesting it be sent to the main saloon.

"I could have sworn we were kindred spirits when it came to kids, but look at you," Kyrkos snorted as they went down the elevator. "What's it like? Being a father?"

Leon wanted to choke out a laugh and say, *Ask me when I've been doing it longer than five minutes*. At the same time, he grew self-conscious with the knowledge he wasn't one. Not really. Which bothered him for some reason.

He couldn't explain that twinge any more than he could explain this well of concern for a baby he'd met barely twenty-four hours ago. He wasn't a sentimental person and certainly hadn't had much role modeling when it came to nurturing. Illi was very small and helpless, though. Everything Tanja had told him about her plight, losing the mother who had essentially sacrificed her own life to give her daughter hers, sat heavily on him, prompting an empathy at her loss despite the fact his own mother was alive and well.

Besides, who wouldn't want to calm an agitated baby? Any decent person would want to feed a helpless, hungry baby whether it was a kitten or puppy or infant. As far as magnanimity went, it wasn't a huge effort to pat her back and speak reassurances. It certainly didn't deserve all this cogitation and remarking upon.

"You didn't want kids?" he asked as a diversion from Kyrkos's question.

"It's the reason my first marriage fell apart. My time off is precious. When I get a break, I want to spend it on the water or the slopes, not… Well, I guess you're not inconvenienced, are you? Still enjoying life, sailing with a baby." Kyrkos flickered his gaze around the atrium as they came off the elevator. "If you call this 'sailing.'" The curl of his lip was a silent *must be nice*.

Thankfully, a steward forestalled further comments as he hurried toward them with the baby bottle on a tray as if he was serving a flute of champagne.

"The chef made it himself. He said the temperature should be perfect."

Leon shook a drop onto the inside of his wrist to be sure, then offered the bottle to Illi.

She took it greedily, smiling around it, which made his mouth twitch. Didn't take much to be a hero in her eyes, did it? He smiled back.

Kyrkos noticed the baby's effect on him. He snorted again, which made Leon defensive of his growing connection with Illi. Something aggressive rose in him, a protectiveness that bordered on irrational since he had a vision of throwing Kyrkos off his yacht.

Leon dragged his attention to the steward. "Where can we find the doctor's wife?"

"The pub, sir."

The bar in the stern was one deck down and meant for casual gatherings and cocktails before dinner. There was abundant seating and it offered potpies and burgers with its vast selection of beer. The three screens of satellite television were invariably tuned to sports.

"Oh. My. Gawd. You have a *baby*?" Cameron rushed toward them as they appeared. She quickly snapped a photo of Leon before he'd realized she was turning her phone on him.

"If you want to take my photo, *ask*," he said, barely keeping his temper.

"Cammy, don't post anything unless Leon says he doesn't mind," Kyrkos hurried to caution her.

"Oops." She winced a sorry-not-sorry. "I already posted, like, a million of the boat."

"The yacht is fine. Delete the one of me and Illi." Leon managed to keep a civil tone. Barely. Tanja hadn't approved such a thing, and he was genuinely incensed by the young woman's utter disregard of their privacy.

"Do I have to?" Cameron batted her lashes. "It's *really* cute."

"I was planning to thank your husband for the house call by arranging for you both to spend a week aboard *Poseidon's Crown* later this year." He let the threat of that rug being pulled hang in the balance.

"That's more than generous compensation for my time," Dr. Kyrkos said, giving his wife's phone a stern nod. "Delete the photo, Cammy."

"If you insist, Kiki." She pouted and tapped her phone. Thankfully, they departed moments later.

Tanja tried to go back to sleep, but when an hour had passed and Leon hadn't returned with Illi, she rose grumpily and put on a robe to go looking for them.

She got lost twice, mostly because there were two dining rooms and she confused them on the map. When she bumped into a steward, he made a call, then offered to make her a fruit smoothie before giving her directions up one deck and forward.

She sipped as she walked to the music salon, contemplating suitably cutting remarks about the yacht having a live concert stage for pop stars. She walked in to find Leon with Illi on his lap, sitting on the bench before the grand piano.

"You have to push harder," he coaxed. "Can you do it?" He stuck his finger against the key she slapped, depressing it enough to make a soft *plink*. "Hear that? You try."

Both of Tanja's ovaries burst into song, throwing sunshine and confetti into the air while her bones softened in a giant, melting, *Awww*.

"They said you were giving her piano lessons." Her rueful voice wasn't quite as nonchalant as she was striving for. "I didn't believe it."

Leon glanced up, looking tired, but he'd cleaned up around his beard and wore a fresh shirt. "She was losing at roulette. I had to get her out of the casino."

"You do *not* have a casino." As she said it, she silently went all in that he did.

"I'd show you, but it's black-tie." He gave her robe a flickering once-over, gaze lingering an extra second on her bare ankles, just long enough to make her very aware that she wore only his T-shirt beneath the warm velour.

And that he'd always been a fan of her long legs.

Illi squawked with excitement at the sight of Tanja, little arms waving, making Tanja smile.

"That's quite a greeting." She set aside her smoothie and came forward to take her.

Her robe loosened and gaped. She fiddled with it before she gathered her daughter and nuzzled Illi's cheek, using the baby as a shield against whatever vibes Leon was throwing off that she was picking up so acutely.

Seriously, any virile man with a baby was going to be a straight shot of pair-bonding chemicals to a woman's inner cave girl. She shouldn't let this affect her so deeply.

"You're wearing fresh clothes," she noted of Illi's onesie. "Who changed you?" She glanced at Leon, expecting him to mention a maid or the doctor's wife.

"I did."

"Really? Why?"

"Her diaper blew out."

"You changed her *diaper*?"

"Why is that so astonishing?" He looked affronted.

"I didn't think you would know how."

"I called the chief engineer to walk me through it."

"Oh. Does she have kids?"

"I was being sarcastic," he said with exasperation. "He's an unmarried man who probably hasn't seen a kid since he was one. No, Tanja, I managed it all by myself. It's not rocket science. Take off the dirty one, swab the deck, put on a clean one. Her pajama thing was stained so I changed that, too. What did I miss?"

Diaper cream, but they'd run out ages ago. Thankfully, Illi's rash hadn't been too bad lately.

"I didn't expect you to be such a natural is all," Tanja said, mildly defensive since he was taking to caring for a baby like it was the easiest thing in the world. She and Brahim had had quite a few misadventures in the early days.

"It's all online," Leon muttered, then abruptly changed the subject with a nod toward her smoothie.

"Were you hungry? You didn't have to leave the room. Dial zero for anything you need."

"When you didn't bring her back, I wanted to know where she was." She craned her neck to avoid Illi's grab for her nose.

He narrowed his eyes. "What did you think? That I gave her to the doctor to leave on a church doorstep or something? Didn't you trust me?"

She pinched her lips, wondering why *that* was so astonishing. "Can you blame me?"

She sank into a chair, still very weak, especially with Illi so energetic and wiggly. She was happily bouncing her legs in frog kicks while twisting and grabbing for anything she could touch.

"But I'm her *father*, Tanja." Leon's tone was so serrated, he could have sliced bread with it. "Surely you believe I could only have her best interests at heart?"

"So do I," she said, guilty of involving him without his consent, but he would wait the rest of his life for her to apologize for that. "You saw how difficult things have become on Istuval. Do you think I should have left her behind at an orphanage? Should I have asked Kahina to raise her when she can't work to support herself and will be living on her brother's generosity for the foreseeable future?"

He glanced away, grimly admitting, "No." He rose and brought her smoothie across, leaving it on a table within reach. "But you've put me in a difficult position."

"Have I? Gosh, that's a shame." She met his gaze. She could speak sarcasm, too.

Leon didn't move, only stood over her, hands

pushed into the pockets of his jeans, not a whiff of humor about him.

She crossed her legs, reminded by his cold, steely stare that she wasn't wearing a stitch of her own clothing and was only off Istuval thanks to him. Her baby was dry and fed when she was in no shape to care for her. Illi was *hers*, also thanks to him.

"I'll quit taking cheap shots," she conceded begrudgingly. "But an explanation would be nice. You quit taking my calls. Did I do something to make you drop me cold like that?"

She subtly braced herself, having convinced herself long ago that his abandonment was somehow her fault and she was too dumb to see it.

"Are we doing this now? All right." He paced away a few restless steps, hands still pushed into his pockets. "You must have seen the reports on how my father's empire collapsed when he did?"

"And that you had to restructure, yes. I understand you were busy, Leon. I'm talking about five minutes to write an email so I wasn't left wondering why you didn't want to come back." Or want to be married to her anymore. He hadn't wanted to even *talk* to her.

She had thought about climbing on a plane to confront him, but she'd been as broke as her brother and father. Leon clearly hadn't wanted to see her, so she had moved on with her life. More or less. She had focused on attaining her degree to avoid dwelling on the happily-ever-after dream she had lost. The money was one thing, the blow to her inner belief system and self-esteem quite another.

"The reports that were made public were the tip of the iceberg." His shoulders became a tense line. "I was doing everything I could to keep the worst of it out of the news. Things were happening very quickly and there was no bottom to the well. Each time I thought about calling you, my situation was worse than it had been an hour before. I couldn't risk revealing any of it and having it become public."

"And you have the nerve to question *my* lack of trust in *you*? I wouldn't have said a word if you'd asked me not to. What can you tell me now? Because silence leaves me making up stories and, believe me, you do not come off well in any of them."

"No?" he asked with derision, but his cheek ticked. "What terrible things have I done?"

"You bankrupted my father's marina."

"Your brother bankrupted it," he responded swiftly and firmly.

"You promised Zach you would invest with him."

"And then I told him I had no money and he should find someone else."

"No money?" she scoffed, looking wildly around at the polished brass and leather upholstery and *grand piano.* "Zach partnered with *you*, Leon. In good faith because he trusted you. And you completely screwed him over. *All of us.*"

"I had every intention of working on the expansion when he proposed it. Once I realized how bad things were with Dad's finances, I had to stage a fire sale. That's business, Tanja. It wasn't personal and he knew that."

Tanja could only stare at him while Illi did squats in her lap, babbling against her fist.

"Zach took it personally," she finally managed to choke out. "We all did. *I* thought your defection was pretty personal, considering we were *married.* I was your *wife*, Leon."

"For a week," he scoffed. "Not even. And it wasn't a real marriage."

That hit her so hard she recoiled into the chair, quickly hugging the baby so she didn't let Illi slide right out of her arms since they seemed to have turned to rubber.

Leon flashed a scowl and moved toward her.

She looked away, blindly staring at the horizon of blue on blue through the huge picture windows. "Silly me, coming all this way to ask for a divorce when we only needed to clap three times and wish it away like a bad dream."

"The marriage was legal. Obviously," he said tersely. "And we are overdue to discuss divorce, I agree with you on that. But it's not as if we were in love, Tanja. We got married because your brother found out I'd slept with you. He said your father would expect it if I was buying into the marina."

"*That's* why you proposed?" Boy, he really knew how to kick someone when they were down.

"You knew that," he said with impatience. Then, after a beat, he added, "Didn't you?"

"Well, I thought you felt *something* for me." She swallowed, trying to clear the croak from her voice. "We were sleeping togeth— Oh, my God." She closed her eyes, hugging the baby and wishing she had the strength to rise and storm off. "You didn't even want to marry me. That's what you're saying, isn't it? I'm such an idiot. I mean, I kind of got that message after you didn't come back, but I thought I had done something to change your mind. Or that you realized you could have had anyone and decided I was too plebian and boring. When you proposed, we had already slept together. I thought that meant you cared about *me*, not just getting me into bed."

"*You* got *me* into bed. You showed up with wine. I wasn't your first lover. I didn't seduce you." He shot each word at her, blunt and fast, then paused, giving her space to correct him.

She couldn't. He was right, much to her chagrin.

"That doesn't explain why you bothered to propose," she choked.

"When big brother twisted my arm... Hell, I don't know why I gave in. I liked Zach." He shrugged. "We were going into business together. Marrying his sister seemed like a good way to secure my side of things. Honestly? Call me delusional, but I didn't think you would accept. I thought we were having a summer fling. You said you were going back to school."

"You bluffed and I called it? That's what you're saying?" she asked with disbelief.

"Pretty much. And there were things with my parents... My father wanted me to come and work for him. I thought a wife and my own business in Canada would get him off my back."

"So I was a bulletproof vest? Did your father know

he was sick? And that things were falling apart? Is that why he wanted you there?" She frowned. "Did *you* know he was sick?"

"It was the sort of massive heart attack that was inevitable, given his lifestyle, but no, none of us knew he was on the verge of one. He hadn't seen a doctor in years. I thought he was being his overbearing self, demanding I come work for him so he could tell me I wasn't doing it right." His expression shuttered. "He'd done that twice before. I wasn't interested in going through it again."

"You must have had mixed feelings, though, after it happened. Must have wished you'd returned when he asked." Any child would. "Is that why you stayed once you got there?"

"I wouldn't have made a different choice if I had realized he was going to die," Leon said dispassionately. "I had made up my mind I wouldn't work for him. That I would start doing my own thing. He was the most entitled bastard you'd never want to meet."

It was such a harsh indictment she could only blink in shock.

She recalled Leon being oddly stoic when he'd taken his mother's call that his father had died. *She insists I come home. I'll be back soon.* It had been eerie, the way he'd taken the news without emotion and acted as though his mother wanting him home was an imposition. Everyone grieved differently, she had told herself, trying not to judge.

That had come later, when he'd ignored her calls and texts.

"I was a different man then." Leon scrubbed a hand across his face. "Spoiled. As long as my credit cards worked, I didn't ask where the money came from. When I was forced to take over, I realized why he had micromanaged me in the past. He was hiding the fact his fortune had been built on things like child labor, collusion, and skirting environmental rules."

"Are you serious?" She absently caught Illi's hand, keeping her fingers from trying to get into her mouth since her jaw was hanging open in shock.

"Completely," he said grimly. "That left me with two choices. I could walk away and lose absolutely everything, leave my mother destitute, and forever wonder if the industrial leaders who moved into our place took a more conscientious approach, or I could do things better myself. They weren't my crimes, but I had benefited from them. I had to clean it up. With great power comes great responsibility, but in order to take responsibility, I had to maintain the power. Understand? So I stayed and made the hard choices that kept us afloat—including backing out of my deal with your brother."

In a twisted way, she saw the logic, and something else. "You couldn't tell me that because you thought I'd go public with it? Spill the beans on your father's misdeeds?"

"We barely knew each other. Frankly, I expected you to come after me for a divorce settlement. The longer time went on and you didn't, the more I thought it was best to let sleeping dogs—"

She narrowed her eyes. He abandoned that met-aphor.

"I figured you knew I was broke and chose to dis-tance yourself. Given the crimes my father had com-mitted, walking away from a wife who didn't want me and an investment opportunity I couldn't afford was nothing by comparison."

"It wasn't 'nothing' to us," she said in a raw voice.

"I didn't tell Zach to move as fast as he did," he de-fended sharply. "He got in way over his head without ensuring his financing was in place. I've had hand-shake deals fall into the toilet myself. That's business, Tanja."

"Yes, I can see how difficult things have been for you. It's not personal that you saved your own butt, not ours. Don't worry about it."

"Oh, climb off your high horse. If I was so terrible, why didn't you divorce me? Why did you even marry me? Love?" he taunted.

"At least that's what I thought it was!" A hot sting of embarrassment rushed across every inch of her skin. "I was young and romantic enough to think passion was a sign of something more enduring. It didn't hurt that my brother thought you were wonder-ful. Everyone wants their spouse to be friends with their sibling. Your investment would have given my dad a very comfortable retirement. My marrying you wrapped everything into a tidy bow of happily-ever-after, so of course I thought you were making all my dreams come true."

He snorted.

"I know that was immature and unrealistic! It still hurts that you didn't even feel that much toward me. Why did you bother coming to Istuval? You could have left me there to rot, never to darken your doorway again."

His expression hardened to granite. He was silent so long she feared she had overstepped in some way. Then he blinked and said, "I thought it would put me in the best position for negotiating our divorce."

That launched a fresh wave of outrage. "I don't want your stupid money, Leon. I just want to be free of you."

"Well, that's a little complicated now, isn't it?" He nodded at Illi, who was standing in her lap, singing in her ear.

"Not really," Tanja said stiffly. "I spent five years living my life without you despite your name being attached to mine on a piece of paper. It will be the same for Illi." She cradled the baby's warm hair and kissed her sweet-smelling cheek. "We don't need anything from you after this little pleasure cruise. I did bookkeeping on the side through school. Once I'm home, I'll hustle up some clients and support us fine. It's what I was going to do anyway."

"I'll give you a settlement," he growled.

A smart woman would snap that up. She had a child to feed. But she was too insulted.

"It wasn't a real marriage," she reminded with an overbright smile. "Let's not turn it into a real divorce."

CHAPTER FOUR

IN ANOTHER LIFE, Leon would have seen Tanja's refusal of his money as a best outcome and moved on. Today, he was incensed.

Before he could open his mouth with a retort, however, the phone in his shirt pocket vibrated. He glanced down and tilted it to see the screen.

"Zach is texting. I'll see if he'll accept a video call." He withdrew the phone and tapped to place the call, then handed the phone to Tanja.

A smile of anticipation burst across her face, sunny with the stark love that she and her family seemed to express unreservedly toward one another. That affection was so constant and raw it was like a force of nature—the kind of thing Leon admired and respected, but didn't trust. Thunder and lightning were exciting to watch, but it would kill you if you were careless enough to be stuck in it unprotected.

"Oh, it's you." Zach's edgy voice eased into surprised relief. "I was worried when I saw Leon wanted a face call. I thought he might have bad news. It's so good to see you."

"Didn't you get the message that we're safe? Illi, look. Say hi to Uncle Zach." She shifted the baby into sitting on her lap to face the camera.

"Hey, sweetheart," Zach said warmly. "Good grief, she's getting big. Well, I hurried out here to take this call, but since it's you…shh." His voice dropped to a whisper, raising hackles of suspicion across Leon's shoulders. "Shonda's sleeping, but look." After a pause, he whispered, "This is Bryant."

"Oh, Zach," Tanja gasped softly. "He's so beautiful."

Her gaze came up, so shiny with joy it shot an arrow straight into Leon's chest, leaving an ache that thrummed a vibration through him. She nodded an invitation for him to come see.

He didn't know why he went. He and Zach were barely speaking, but he moved to stand behind Tanja and saw a newborn swaddled in a yellow blanket and wearing a pale green hat.

"Congratulations," Leon said politely.

"Oh. You are there." Zach's tone went flat with dismay. The image jostled as he slipped from the hospital room out into the hall, then the screen flipped to show Zach's disheveled hair and weary face. "Thank you for getting Tanja off Istuval. Shonda was on bed rest and had an emergency C-section yesterday."

"Everything went okay?" Tanja asked anxiously.

"They're both doing really well."

"I can't wait to hold him," Tanja sighed.

"I thought you'd be on a plane." Zach frowned. "I was texting for a flight number. Where are you?"

"On Leon's yacht."

"Tanja isn't well enough to fly," Leon said.

"I can fly," she insisted, sending a disgruntled look over her shoulder at him.

"You can barely fight the baby for the phone." Illi was about to win in her quest to grab it so he plucked her from Tanja's lap, telling Zach, "Tanja and I have some legal things to sort out. We'll do that in Athens and let you know her plans from there."

"Finally getting a divorce? Good idea," Zach said in a cool voice that grew concerned as he asked Tanja. "What happened? How did you get sick?"

Leon moved across to a colorful abstract painting, giving Illi something to stare at while Tanja reassured her brother that she had seen a doctor and was already feeling better.

Leon was replaying her accusation that he had destroyed her brother financially. Was that how Zach viewed it?

It didn't hurt that my brother thought you were wonderful. Everyone wants their spouse to be friends with their sibling.

Leon hadn't worried too much about terminating their business deal. For starters, he hadn't had a choice, and as much as he'd liked Zach, he hadn't felt deep loyalty toward him. Growing up with seemingly unlimited wealth, toys, looks and freedom meant that Leon had always attracted a lot of friends, most of whom wanted to take advantage of their association with him.

Leon had met Zach when he'd hired him as a tactician after losing to a team Zach had navigated through the San Juans. Such a tight working relationship demanded a lot of communication and reliance so they'd come to know each other fairly well, but Leon had been stung by hangers-on in the past. He only opened up as much as was absolutely necessary.

Zach's pitch for a marina expansion had been nothing new. Leon had been drawn in because Zach had been dropping off the racing circuit to take over his father's business. It was the complete opposite of something Leon would allow himself to be pressured into. He'd been deeply selfish in those days. There'd been a part of him that had imagined if he helped Zach he'd have an angle to persuade him to keep racing. That's how Leon had been raised to view the world—favors begat favors. There was nothing money couldn't buy. Nothing was done out of genuine caring or friendship.

Learning Tanja blamed him for the loss of her father's business left a metallic taste of dishonor in his mouth. Especially when it had come about because he'd dumped Zach's deal to rescue his own father's business—a business built on lies and cheated negotiations.

Leon *hated* to see anything of his father in himself, but that tainted blood showed up at different times in ways that never ceased to make him loathe himself. Hell, he was so much like his old man that his wife felt scorned and tricked by him, the same way his mother had always felt about his father.

I thought you felt something for me. We were sleeping together.

Leon had felt toward Tanja what he had felt toward

any attractive, available woman who reciprocated his interest—sexual desire. Granted, it had been an acute level of that sort of interest. Before meeting her, he'd had relationships of various lengths from one-night stands to yearlong affairs. All had been pleasant, and none had inspired more than basic levels of affection.

Tanja had been different. Obvious in her interest, which was always a kick for a man's ego, but mesmerizing in how she was both playful and earnest. Sincere.

Leon had known deep down that she took things more seriously than he did. The connection between her and Zach and their father was infinitely more complex and *real* than anything he could begin to comprehend. Being around them had been both fascinating and puzzling. Intimidating in some ways because it was one of the few things in life he knew he would never grasp or properly experience.

Leon had known in his gut that having an affair with Tanja would lead her on, which was probably why he'd wound up proposing. He'd been convinced they wouldn't last, that she would eventually figure out he wasn't capable of giving her the emotional depth she expected, but he'd wanted her anyway.

And she had been a grown woman capable of making her own decisions. That's how he'd rationalized it. In reality, he'd wanted to sleep with a woman who appealed to him. That's what kind of man he'd been— not devoid of conscience, but with a very superficial grasp of right and wrong. Not much sense of consequence, either. All that had mattered was getting what—or who—he wanted when he wanted them.

He'd grown up since then. Now he considered what was best for other people, not just himself.

Finally getting a divorce? Good idea, Zach had said a minute ago.

It was. But something in Leon balked. He was a champion at heart. That's why he'd won more races than he'd lost. That's how he'd pulled his father's company back from the brink. A stubborn refusal to fail wasn't much use when one party wanted to end things, though. He knew what it looked like when people who resented one another stayed married. He couldn't do that to himself, or Tanja, or the baby who rested her head on his shoulder.

He absently rubbed Illi's back, listening to Tanja wrap up with her brother.

"Let Dad know I'm fine. Tell him I'll call soon."

"I will. Love you, Books."

"Love you, too. All three of you." She ended with a happy sigh and set aside the phone to hug herself. "I'm an auntie. How amazing is that?"

Technically, that made Leon an uncle, but he didn't allow that flitting thought to land and take root.

Tanja sipped her smoothie, then frowned.

"Not sitting well?"

"Just a lump of banana that surprised me." She took another sip and made a face. "I really am feeling a lot better. I think some of it was seasickness."

He came across to touch her forehead. She wasn't feverish.

Illi smiled and reached for her, making Tanja smile. "Hi, baby doll. Come here."

That brightness was back in her face. A woman in makeup and heels was undeniably attractive, but Tanja, fresh faced and wearing nothing but confidence and the sheen of unconditional love, was spellbinding.

He had an urge to cup her cheek and caress her soft skin with his thumb. He wanted her to look at *him* with that warm, unabashed smile.

Disturbed, he made himself give her the baby and picked up his phone.

"Don't try to rush your recovery. You've been through a lot." He had already relayed to staff that she needed supplements. He would ask them to add some rich desserts to the menu, too. She could stand to gain a few kilos.

"I don't want to rely on you any longer than necessary. Kahina was so generous and understanding, but you know what they say about houseguests."

He lifted his gaze.

"They're like fish. They start to stink after three days."

"Is that what they say?" He smirked as he went back to checking his emails. "Well, I've asked my lawyer to fly out to join u—" He swore as three different subject lines jumped out at him, all running a variation of *You're married?*

"What's wrong?"

"Secret is out on our marriage." He explained that Cameron had been posting photos of the yacht. "She must have said something about being aboard so her husband could check on my wife."

"So much for patient confidentiality. Why did you tell him we were married?"

"What else was I supposed to say?"

"I don't know." Her mouth pulled with uncertainty. "What does it mean? Will anyone care?"

"I am quoted and photographed from time to time," he said drily. More on the business side, not as much on his pursuit of pleasure since he'd given up chasing women and regatta trophies, but he was a rich and powerful man. Did she not realize that?

She was frowning with worry, smoothing her hand over Illi's hair.

"It's a scoop, not a scandal," he reassured her. "I'll talk to my PR team, release a statement." He shrugged it off. Even as he did, his phone pinged twice more. A fresh email from the head of a media conglomerate asked if he knew a photo of him with his baby was being shopped to news outlets.

Leon *really* swore.

"What?" Tanja asked, eyes popping with growing alarm.

"She didn't delete the photo with Illi." And this was why he hadn't seen the value in Zach's friendship when Zach had offered it. Leon had known Kyrkos most of his life, but the doctor was throwing away their lifelong relationship for what? Five minutes of fame for his status-seeking wife?

Tanja closed her arms around Illi. "But if it's reported that we have a baby, what if it comes out that our situation isn't entirely—"

"Legal?" he charged.

"By the book," she corrected. She bit her lip before closing her eyes and turning her nose into Illi's cheek. Her brow furrowed with deep anxiety. Fear of losing her baby.

That revelation of such deep vulnerability made the pit of his stomach churn with a primal compulsion to protect.

"My lawyer, Georgiou, is arriving tomorrow." His voice was a bass echo from deep in his chest. "I'll put him onto ensuring t's are crossed and i's dotted where Illi is concerned."

Tension lingered around her mouth, but she spoke decisively. "Take me to Malta. I want to fly home." Her voice caught on the word "home." "If I'm there—"

"You can't *get* home," he reminded her. "Illi doesn't have a passport. Customs agents will ask if you have permission from her father to take her overseas. They'll want to see her paperwork and it's not up to scrutiny."

"Write me a letter that says you give us permission," she demanded. "*I'll* write one."

"Another false document? Great idea. No, Tanja. I'm not like my father. I keep my nose clean, along with the rest of my life." He was terse now, annoyed that she was resisting his help. "Given the choice between throwing fuel on a messy story about abandoning my baby to my estranged wife or a very nice story about my wife and I starting a family, I'm going with the nice one."

"Oh, that lie is fine? She's not *yours*, Leon!"

"Check the paperwork *you* filed," he snapped.

She flinched with hurt and looked away, mouth trembling but jaw pugnacious.

He pushed his hand through his hair as he gathered his patience. "Look, I believe it's in Illi's best interest for her to be with you. I'm not going to let anyone take her from you. You have my word on that."

"Forgive me if I don't think your promises are reliable."

Maybe he deserved that, but it still cut like a whip.

"Like it or not, *you* made me responsible for her. I won't shirk that responsibility." He was *not* like his father, disregarding the needs of a child—his own son included—because it suited him. "You and I butting heads every minute won't help."

"I wish I'd never m—" She sealed her lips over whatever she'd been about to say.

"Met me? Married me? Then you wouldn't have Illi, would you?" he summed up brutally.

He took the baby from her, something she was too weak to prevent, and she could utter only a disgruntled sound.

"I'll keep her while you rest. Do you want to sleep here? On a lounger by the pool? I can help you back to the stateroom if you need it."

She looked between him and the baby, her body trembling with anger.

"I've spent a lot of time thinking you're a selfish

jerk who is ruthless about getting what he wants. This doesn't change my opinion." She pushed to her feet and lost all her haughty air of superiority when she paled and had to hang on to the chair.

He steadied her, but she shook him off.

"Bring her up when she's ready for her nap."

"Of course," he said, because he might be selfish and ruthless, but he was also capable of magnanimity—once he got what he wanted.

Tanja woke with a sense she wouldn't fall back asleep. Not only had she been sleeping on and off for nearly twenty-four hours, but her mind leaped into a whirl of wondering what would happen now that her marriage was public. What would happen with her adoption of Illi? It was still so tentative.

She didn't want to rely on Leon and his lawyers to sort things, but what choice did she have? Her financial resources were depleted, and she couldn't work until she at least had a laptop and an internet connection. She couldn't buy anything until she had some income. It was a catch-22.

"Why are you sighing like that? Are you in pain?"

Leon's quiet voice beside her made her gasp and roll over, realizing as she did that he was lying on top of the covers beside her.

"What are you doing here?"

"Sleeping. Until you started huffing and puffing. Do you need a house blown down or something?"

"I'm just restless. Frustrated."

He left a nice round silence for her to hear the suggestiveness of her own words.

"By my situation," she clarified. "Jeez, seriously?"

"I didn't say a thing," he said mildly, but she had the sense he was laughing at her. He curled his arm beneath his pillow. He still wore the clothes he'd been wearing earlier, but she saw the pale glow of his bare feet in the dim light.

"You could have gone to bed properly. Somewhere else," she pointed out.

"This is *my* bed," he said drily. "The sofa is too short and I need to be able to hear Illi so you don't have to get up. You didn't even notice me here. Go back to sleep."

"She's in the lounge?" She lifted her head and cocked her ear, but their talking didn't seem to be disturbing her. "Thank you for helping me look after her."

"She said begrudgingly," he mocked, voice still low with sleepy amusement.

"I do resent needing your help," she admitted. "But you have to admit this is strange."

"That you've woken me to *talk*? Yes."

That caused such a stab of memory, of slithering against him in the night, naked skin brushing as their limbs twined, she made a noise of injury that she hoped he assumed was an impatient tsk.

"I forgot that you were up all last night. I'm sorry I woke you," she said stiffly, and rolled so her back was to him.

"I've been asleep since Illi went down at seven. It's fine." The humor was gone from his voice and now it was tinged with something more serious. Conciliatory, perhaps. "What do you think is strange? That we're five years fake married and now we're faking that we have a baby together? It wasn't on my bucket list, I'll say that."

She rolled back to face him even though she couldn't see him in the dark. "Haven't you wanted to…find someone else and get started on a family of your own?"

"No," he said, low and prompt and unequivocal. "I never wanted kids."

"Wow." And ouch. She hadn't expected such a strong response when he was actually very sweet with Illi. "I'm sorry we're imposing then."

"You're not. My childhood was lousy. That's all. I'm sure I told you that."

He had, but he had always deflected when she tried to pry anything more out of him.

"From the outside, it looks as though you had everything you wanted. I was always surprised to hear you call your childhood 'lousy.'"

"On the surface, I did have everything." He sounded resentful, but she didn't think it was directed at her. "The best food and clothes. Travel and education. It should have been ideal, but my parents' marriage was horrific. That skewed my view of family. I never wanted to subject a child to that tension and manipulation."

"I guess I should have asked if you wanted kids before we married. I always saw myself as getting married and having children. We really were doomed, weren't we?"

There was a profound silence before he said, quietly but powerfully, "I thought so."

That sent another knifing pain through her. "My God, Leon! Why did you even go through with it?"

"I told you. I wanted to get my father off my back."

"That's so *cold*."

"I'm being honest, Tanja. As honest as I should have been back then. Maybe if I had, you wouldn't have married me. Did you really believe we'd have the picket fence, two kids and a dog? End up in side-by-side rocking chairs on the porch?"

"First of all, we should be so lucky as to grow old at all." She bunched the edge of the blanket beneath her chin, thinking of her father losing her mother when they'd been so devoted to one another. "I didn't think marriage would be easy, but I thought we'd figure things out as we went along. Mom and Dad got married really fast and had challenges, but they found ways to get through them. They went into it intending to make their life together and made it seem doable, if not simple. That's what commitment is, right? Committing to figuring out how to stay together while working through stuff?"

"Why did they marry so quickly?" His head turned on the pillow. "Was she pregnant with Zach?"

"The opposite." She couldn't help the gossipy chuckle that came into her throat. "They both had really strict parents and were saving themselves for marriage, but couldn't wait so they had a short engagement. Isn't that cute?"

Leon didn't say anything.

"Do *not* say I should have done the same thing."

"I wasn't going to."

"What then?"

Nothing.

"Some things never change." She was hurt by his silence. She really should have seen how doomed they were from the way he had always shut her out like this. She had tried to give him space, thinking he would let down his guard eventually, but they hadn't had time and apparently he still didn't want to open up.

He suddenly came up on his elbow, looming over her. His imposing silhouette pressed her deep into the mattress. There was only a slanting glow from the other room, making it impossible to read his expression.

"I haven't been with anyone since you." He threw the words down like a gauntlet.

"Liar." It was too flabbergasting.

"Believe what you want." He sounded insulted. "It's the truth."

She wouldn't normally be so rude, but the man had been a sexual animal.

"Did something happen?" she asked with sudden concern. "Are you okay?"

"My mojo is *fine*, Tanja." Definitely insulted. "It was a *choice*."

"Really." She couldn't help that she was so skeptical. "Why would you do that? Or *not* do it."

The silhouette of his profile looked to whatever moonlight was sparkling on the distant ripples of the sea.

"I had already done enough things that made me like my father. He had committed so many atrocities... Infidelity felt like the last tawdry straw. If I could hang on to a shred of moral character, if I kept myself from doing that one thing, then for sure I was a step above the human garbage that he was."

His view of himself was so bleak it made her unutterably sad. "So celibacy was like...a form of self-flagellation?"

"Oh, yeah, I've done a lot of that," he assured her with a ripple of self-deprecating amusement in his tone.

She burst out laughing and shoved at his shoulder, not moving him an inch. "Is that what the kids are calling it these days?"

"I wouldn't know. No one admits to doing it." His teeth flashed.

This, she thought with a warm glow. This was the man who had so dazzled her that she had been unable to say anything but yes to his proposal. She'd been willing to do anything he suggested. The things they'd done on his sailboat? Whew.

She grew very aware of the rumpled blankets between them and the intimacy of the low light and the warmth off his body. His scent and solid strength. His weight tipping her toward him on the mattress.

Maybe that was simply his magnetism pulling at her.

He was looking at her. When he spoke, his tone was somber.

"It's fine that you've had lovers while we were still married." He smoothed a wrinkle from the blanket between them. "I didn't expect you to be faithful. That was my own baggage I was working through."

"I…" Was she really going to admit this? "What makes you think I've had lovers?"

A silence crashed over them, so loud it might have been a five-alarm fire bell.

"Why wouldn't you? You don't need punishing," he said evenly.

She folded her fingers over the edge of the blanket, loath to admit what a spell he'd cast, one so strong she was still under it.

"Tanja." He sounded so grave he made her heart shiver in her chest. When his finger looped to pick up a tendril of her hair, a tingling sensation swept down her nape into her breast. "Please don't tell me I hurt you so badly that you couldn't trust men. If you denied yourself the pleasure of sex because…" He swallowed. "It really would be too much for even my fairly impervious conscience to bear."

"It wasn't that." She licked her lips, hyperaware of his finger twirling that length of hair. "I mean, I was pretty disenchanted with men and the institution of marriage, but I had to work while I was in school. I didn't have time to do more than go for coffee. Anything more than that would have meant I'd have to free myself of you first and…"

This part was hard to admit because Leon had set a certain bar. No one had made her feel the way she was feeling right now, and he was only touching her hair. Since when were there electrical currents in strands of hair that ran straight to erogenous zones, lighting her up like a Christmas display?

"I never met anyone who—" *tempted me the way*

you did "—seemed worth going to the trouble of filing the papers. You didn't break me, Leon."

"Good," he said after a pulse beat. "I don't want that kind of power."

"Too much responsibility?" she guessed in a voice that was strained by the reactions and emotions she was trying to stifle.

"Yes." He spoke frankly, but gently. His fist was resting on her shoulder and his fingertip extended to play with her ear. "You weren't even tempted to have a casual hookup, though? You're so passionate."

"Not really. Not if I can go five years without sex," she joked weakly.

"You're very passionate. That hasn't changed." His tickling touch dipped into the hollow beneath her ear, making her scalp tighten. "This may come as a surprise to you, but most people do whatever I tell them to do. You've always pushed back on me. It's frustrating, but I have to respect you for it."

"You must bring it out in me." She was trying to keep it light, even though his caress was making runnels of heat invade her limbs. If he knew what was happening beneath these blankets—the flush of sensual heat likely turning her skin pink, the peaked nipples that were stinging with anticipation, the flooding heat settling in an ache between her thighs—he would be on her like a wolf on a fawn.

"We do seem to play off one another, don't we? I haven't forgotten." It was a smoky warning that made her want to wriggle closer.

She pushed her palm against the weight of the

blanket where his chest was radiating warmth into
her side, resisting him as much as reminding herself
that she ought to.

"Easy, sailor. After five years, I'm thinking a stiff
breeze is all you need to get excited. Don't pretend
your reaction has anything to do with me."

"See, that makes me think *you've* forgotten how
good we are together."

He hadn't moved, and she was suddenly fixated on
how close he was, willing him to close the distance
between his mouth and hers.

She should have said something pithy, but wound
up saying, "Perhaps I have."

And slowly, very, very slowly, the shadow of his
shoulders shifted. His head lowered. The tip of his
nose brushed hers and the heat of his lips settled
feathery soft across hers. She let her mouth open
slightly while he ever so gently deepened the contact,
searching out the fit before he sealed them in a deep
kiss and plunged them into a molten sea of passion.

She made a throaty noise of shock, expecting playful excitement, not this sharp jab of wanton hunger.
Her breath dried up while her whole body flushed,
accosted by lascivious longing.

He stilled as though their combined reaction startled him, too. Maybe he was weighing whether her
noise had been a protest.

She brought her hand from beneath the covers to
grab his wrist, silently conveying that she wanted
him to keep kissing her.

He pressed into it, opening his mouth wider to rav-
age her unreservedly. His wrist twisted against her

grip and his fingers slid between hers. He pressed her hand onto the pillow beside her head as he let his weight come over her and crush her into the mattress.

She was smothered by his weight, trapped by his bulk and the covers and the way he was making love to her mouth. It was magnificent. She moaned her encouragement, abandoning herself to the madness they conjured.

He made a ragged noise of suffering as he dragged his mouth to nip at her jaw and skate down the side of her neck.

"It's better than I remembered," he said hotly. "You taste so damned good." His mouth came back to bite her earlobe, then suck, sending showering tingles through her. "Stop me."

She only turned her head to seek his mouth with hers. Damn these covers between them. She writhed, pushing her hip against the blunted shape of him. He closed his legs outside hers, trapping her into a tight line pinned beneath him.

She arched to feel more of him, moaning into his mouth as they played their tongues together. She wanted to touch him, *feel* him. Strip naked and take him inside her.

He leaned on one elbow and raked the blankets from between them, down to her waist. His free hand swept up to cup her breast, plumping it against the soft cotton of the T-shirt she wore.

"Seriously. Stop me or I'm going to keep going," he warned in a growl even as he dropped his head and opened his hot mouth over her nipple.

The muted sensation was strong enough she

wanted to lift her knees and curl protectively. She couldn't. She was at his mercy.

The cotton quickly dampened as he lightly bit and sucked at her through the fabric, the attentions sending hot, stabbing sensations into her loins.

At least her arms were free. She roamed her hands greedily across his back, soaking up the heat of his shoulders and biceps through the fabric of his shirt, the hot skin of his neck beneath his collar. She filtered the coarse curls on his head through her fingers and opened her mouth against the soft-rough stubble on his chin.

She wanted to beg him to do filthy things with her. Her body said it for her as she drew him back to kiss her and gave him her tongue.

He blatantly sucked and worked his own against hers, jabbing erotic thrills into her with the flagrant play, drawing more moans from her that echoed against his.

He shifted atop her, allowing her to open her legs beneath the blankets, welcoming his weight between her thighs. He rocked against her as he bit her bottom lip. She lifted her hips into his muted thrusts and clung weakly to him.

"Do you have a—"

Illi began to cry in the other room.

Condom was left unspoken. They were both frozen and pulsating.

Leon swore. He dropped his head into the pillow next to Tanja's ear, panting as though he'd been at the bottom of the sea and finally made it to the surface.

In the next second, he rolled off her, arm across his face to hide his chiseled features.

She weakly pushed her legs toward the edge of the mattress.

"I'll get her," he said in a strained voice. "Just give me a sec."

She was equally addled but desperate to flee. What had just happened? A cataclysm, obviously, but how? Why? What did it mean?

"I'll go." She kicked her way out of the tangled covers and snatched up the robe off the chair. "It's okay, baby doll," she murmured as she made her way through to the lounge. "Mommy's here."

She was still unsteady on her feet, but she didn't think it was remnants of her illness. She had nearly succumbed to Leon's lovemaking, and that was like a near-death experience.

She bent to collect Illi out of the cot and experienced a rush of light-headedness when she came back up.

"I had the chef make a bottle before I put her down for the night," Leon said from the shadows of the corridor, near the door to the head. "It's in the fridge behind the bar. If you can manage her by yourself, I'll shower."

"Of course. Thank you."

He walked into the head and firmly closed the door.

YOU pick your books –
WE pay for everything.
You get up to FOUR New Books and TWO Mystery Gifts...absolutely FREE!

Dear Reader,

I am writing to announce the launch of a huge **FREE BOOK GIVEAWAY**... and to let you know that YOU are entitled to choose up to FOUR fantastic books that WE pay for.

Try **Harlequin® Desire** books featuring the worlds of the American elite with juicy plot twists, delicious sensuality and intriguing scandal.

Try **Harlequin Presents® Larger-Print** books featuring the glamourous lives of royals and billionaires in a world of exotic locations, where passion knows no bounds.

Or TRY BOTH!

In return, we ask just one favor: Would you please participate in our brief Reader Survey? We'd love to hear from you.

This FREE BOOK GIVEAWAY means that we pay for *everything!* We'll even cover the shipping, and no purchase is necessary, now or later. So please return your survey today. You'll get **Two Free Books** and **Two Mystery Gifts** from each series to try, altogether worth over **$20!**

Sincerely

Pam Powers

Pam Powers
For Harlequin Reader Service

Complete the survey below and return it today to receive up to 4 FREE BOOKS and FREE GIFTS guaranteed!

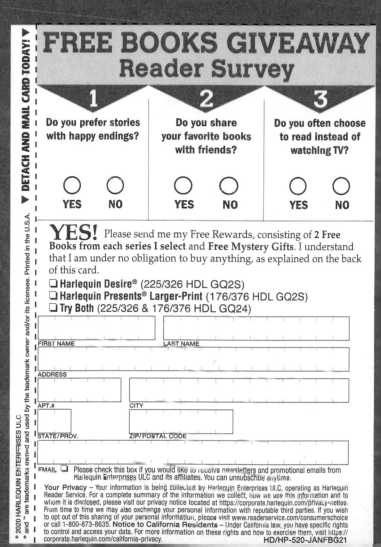

HARLEQUIN READER SERVICE—Here's how it works:

BUSINESS REPLY MAIL
FIRST-CLASS MAIL   PERMIT NO. 717   BUFFALO, NY

POSTAGE WILL BE PAID BY ADDRESSEE

HARLEQUIN READER SERVICE
READER SERVICE
PO BOX 1341
BUFFALO NY 14240-8571

NO POSTAGE
NECESSARY
IF MAILED
IN THE
UNITED STATES

▲ If offer card is missing write to: Harlequin Reader Service, P.O. Box 1341, Buffalo, NY 14240-8531 or visit www.ReaderService.com ▲

CHAPTER FIVE

LEON DISAPPEARED WITHOUT a word after his shower.

Tanja put Illi back down and slept fitfully, waking alone in the stateroom when Illi did. She called down to order Illi's morning bottle, then sang to her as she changed her.

It was such a beautiful morning that Tanja opened one of the doors to the starboard deck, letting the fresh air stream in. They seemed to be at anchor, sheltered near a wall of stone with patches of greenery growing in the steps and crevices. It was stunning, the reflection nearly perfect in the calm blue water.

"Cythera Island," Kyle informed her when he delivered Illi's bottle. "Kýrios Petrakis asked me to relay that his team from Athens will arrive shortly—" He nodded toward the door she'd opened as the growing sound of a helicopter could be heard beyond. "Breakfast will be served on the lido deck if you feel up to joining them. If not, he'll check in with you later."

"That must have been an early start," she noted. "I'll come down as soon as I dress." She was actually starving and anxious to get a grip on how things would proceed.

Plus, she'd rather not face Leon alone. She'd rather not face him at all. Their make-out session had kept her tossing and turning with sexual frustration and mortification. If Illi hadn't interrupted them, she would have made love with him. Tanja kept telling herself deprivation had caused her to react with such abandon, but Leon had lost none of his skill or appeal. One kiss and she'd been right back to the crush that had made her so reckless five years ago.

What he'd ever seen in her remained a mystery. Five years of forgoing carbs made stale bread look really appetizing, she supposed.

No matter why they'd succumbed to impulse, the fact was that the uneasy truce they'd established was impacted. Tanja's sense of who they were, individually and as a couple, had vanished. When she had been able to dismiss him as that jerk who had abandoned her, she had faced him without self-consciousness over whether he found her attractive or liked her. She'd been convinced he felt nothing toward her or he wouldn't have left her.

With the memory of his hands sweeping away the blankets and his mouth chasing across hers, however, she was plunged into overanalyzing and second-guessing. She eyed her crinkle cotton skirt and pale pink sleeveless T-shirt with a wish that she possessed something more flattering—or at least had her old curves to fill out what hung off her like wet laundry on a rack. She was still very pale, her lips almost white, her hair fine and flat.

Was this the real reason he'd forsaken her? Her lack of appeal and sophistication?

Who cared? She wanted him out of her life.

Didn't she?

Leon wasn't as feckless as she'd judged him. He was infuriating in his lack of remorse where Zach and the loss of her father's marina was concerned, but he'd explained enough that she understood better the pressures that had pushed him to act the way he had. The things he'd said about his father were particularly chilling. She was proud of him for trying to make reparations, but the experience had clearly left an indelible scar on him, one that would be with him always.

Her heartache on his behalf didn't change her desire to divest herself of a marriage that was nothing more than a piece of paper, though. She couldn't remain married in name only forever.

The problem was, his passionate kisses had reawakened a desire to have…something. With someone.

Not him, of course. He didn't believe in lifelong commitments and didn't want children.

Illi had finished her bottle and was rolling and squirming, ready to take on the world. Tanja could have stood there angsting over Leon and her appearance for the rest of the day, but she gathered her daughter and searched out the lido deck.

The dining area next to the main swimming pool was sometimes called the beach, Kyle had informed her.

Tanja emerged into the shadow of an awning, but the glare off the pool and the gleaming, polished deck made her squint. The view beyond was open to the stern. Rocky islands rose from an impossibly blue sea, reaching toward a cerulean sky. The salt-scented breeze caught her skirt, playing it against her shins in a tickling caress. Soft notes of a bouzouki came from hidden speakers while casual voices milled over a buffet spread.

"Tanja." Leon broke away to approach her. He wore crisp linen pants in a bone color and a collared T-shirt in rust red. He moved with his usual panther-like grace, stealing her breath. He'd tidied up around his stubble, but she couldn't read his expression, thanks to his mirrored sunglasses. "Good morning."

He casually claimed Illi and lowered his chin to say good morning to the baby in Greek, then caught Illi's hand when she tried to put a palm print on his sunglasses. His thumb tucked into her palm and she curled her tiny fingers over it.

That small gesture undid all the stern lectures Tanja had given herself five minutes ago.

"How are you feeling?" Leon asked her.

For one heart-stopping moment, Tanja thought he was asking about last night. In front of all these people. And everyone stopped what they were doing to look at her as though they were also curious to know how she felt after some heavy petting with her estranged husband.

As her stomach swooped and panged, however, she remembered she was sick.

"Feeling much better," she said in a strangled voice. "No fever. I'm actually quite hungry."

"Good. Let me introduce you." He drew her toward the half-dozen men and women in casual but crisp business wear. A few gave side-eyes at Leon's comfortable wrangling of Illi, but they offered Tanja warm smiles.

"Good morning," Tanja said shyly as she tried to memorize the names of two different lawyers, a PR manager, a photographer, Leon's PA, and a stylist who looked at her the way her brother looked at a salvaged boat—like scraping the seaweed and barnacles would be a ton of work but hopefully worth the effort.

"Help yourself," Leon said to Tanja, nodding at the heaping platters of brunch items.

He moved to where an infant swing had been suspended in the shade near the head of the table and secured Illi into it. He gave it a nudge, and they all laughed at the way Illi squealed and began to happily kick her legs.

Moments later, when Tanja came to the table with her filled plate, Leon loomed beside her, holding the chair closest to Illi, to the left of the head of the table.

His gallantry flustered her. Was he trying to show off?

If he noticed her blush, he didn't let on.

"Kyrkos texted that you don't need antibiotics. Rest, fluids, and vitamins." He nodded at the pill bottle standing next to her water glass.

"Thanks. Did you ask what I should take for the

rage blackout over having my child exploited?" she asked in an undertone.

"Ha." His barked laugh made everyone turn their heads, wanting in on the joke. "I already know what to take for that." The corner of his mouth curled with a lack of mercy. "The sweet serum of revenge. I've already ordered it."

She widened her eyes. "In the form of?"

"I've rescinded my offer to host him and his wife aboard this yacht. Presumably, whatever Cameron gets for the photo is sufficient compensation for his house call. The doctor's ex-wife and her new beau, however, have been invited to enjoy a month aboard *Poseidon's Crown* in the location of their choice."

"Oof." Tanja sat back against the cushions in her chair. "You're not a man to cross, are you?"

"I'm really not," he said with a flinty smile.

Tanja's heart went cold as she remembered *she* had crossed Leon.

"I've spoken to Georgiou about how things were left on Istuval." Leon nodded at the lawyer on his right. "We'll have several meetings through the rest of the day to address how we'll proceed. Eat up."

She looked at the scrumptious tropical fruits and flaky pastries before her, but her appetite was gone.

Leon had managed to keep his hands and lips off women for five years. There had been nights when he'd thought he would go around the bend with sexual frustration, but aside from ogling the occasional pair of legs or a really nice rack, he'd managed to keep his libido firmly leashed.

Until last night when he had completely lost his head.

Was that what celibacy did to a man? Because he shouldn't have gone from zero to a hundred in the space of a sigh. He'd still been catching up on sleep from pulling an all-nighter aboard the trimaran. And he'd been in a terrible mood, peeved about a lot of things, not least that one old friend had betrayed him while the other clearly couldn't stand him. His own hypocrisy annoyed him most of all. He was stung that Zach still resented him over their broken deal, but he had no intention of forgiving the opportunistic doctor for taking advantage of him. Yes, he was a blackened kettle calling out the pot.

When he'd settled on the bed next to Tanja, he had only wanted to turn off his brain and sleep. He hadn't even allowed himself to fall deeply asleep. He'd been listening for the baby so she wouldn't wake Tanja.

Tanja's restlessness had tripped something in him, though. He'd woken in a rush of sexual awareness that he might have ignored if their conversation hadn't turned so intimate.

Why had he felt compelled to tell her he'd been forgoing sex? It wasn't that he felt embarrassed or proud of it. He had never worn sexual conquests as a badge so a lack of them didn't prickle his ego.

But it had been a profoundly intimate thing to reveal. She had said that small thing about her parents and he'd had a flash of admiration for them. Of wishing he was a tiny bit like them instead of so much like his own father.

Then she had practically dared him to prove they still had chemistry, and the next thing he'd known he'd been trying to sate the most powerful sexual hunger he'd ever experienced. He'd been close to losing himself like an adolescent—and they'd had layers of clothing and blankets between them. What would have happened if they'd been naked?

He knew what would have happened. With a flood of heat straight to his groin, he vividly recalled Tanja's pale, lithe form straddling him the first time they'd made love. It was a favorite image in the highlight reel that he had replayed thousands of times since their very short marriage. He had believed it was nothing more than an embellished memory. They'd had fun for a few weeks, but sex with Tanja hadn't been any more profound than his other intimate experiences.

He had clung to that conviction until last night.

Now he was seeing his disinterest in other women in a different light. In the last five years, anytime he'd felt a glimmer of attraction toward someone new, he had reminded himself he was married. That he had scruples.

Did he, though? Or had his instinctual turning away gone deeper?

Those other women hadn't been Tanja. Their hair had been the wrong color. Their laughter too high-pitched or too husky, not the perfect balance of clear and throaty. They had talked about things that should have interested him, but failed to engage him intellectually. They'd projected small signals of receptivity, placing a hand on an arm or tilting a head with invitation, but he'd always been turned off, not on. He'd been aware of the opportunity, but something had stopped him from wanting to cross that line.

Maybe his faithfulness to his marriage vows wasn't about proving he was a better man than his father. Maybe he had imprinted on his wife like one of those animals that mated for life—like a wolf. Or a seahorse. *That* scared the hell out of him.

Marriage was not a ticket to eternal happiness. He knew that. It was a shackle to another person's whims and hurtful behaviors.

Yes, he had let himself believe for five minutes that his own marriage could be different. Tanja had that effect on him. She made everything seem brighter and hotter and softer and sweeter. She was like a club drug—something he avoided because he didn't like the crash landing back into reality.

That's how he'd come down from his marriage, by returning to Greece and discovering that, even in death, his father caused both him and his mother untold anguish.

Leon had proceeded to do the same to his own wife. He'd failed to send the money, hurting Tanja and her whole family. He'd pulled back from her out of shame, grateful that she wasn't striking back. A cold war was better than an active one.

The minute he was back in her sphere, however, she had lobbed a grenade by naming him Illi's father.

Leon was still furious with her for putting his

name on the paperwork without his consent. He'd
been completely honest last night when he had told
her he had never expected to be married with a baby.
Family wasn't something he understood well enough
to imagine he could do it successfully. He was bound
to do more damage than good, and he hated failure.

On top of that, he was facing untold legal trouble
and their clandestine, lusty, expiring marriage was
tumbling into the public eye.

Behind him, Georgiou was trying to forestall the
worst of what might come out. He was interviewing
Tanja, making notes on all the people on Istuval who
might help with changing Illi's paperwork and any
who might threaten the process.

Yet, when Leon heard Tanja ask, "How will our
divorce affect all this?" he spun from the ruminations
he'd been directing out the window overlooking the
view off the stern and came back to rejoin them at
the small conference table in his office.

"We can't divorce," Leon said implacably, skin
too tight because some force within him was pushing outward. "Not until Illi's adoption is finalized.
No one will authorize an adoption to a couple in the
middle of a breakup."

"But we don't know how long the adoption will
take." Tanja looked to Georgiou for guidance. "Do we?"

Georgiou shook his head with regret. "A month?
A year? We'll need patience and diplomacy so the
authorities on Istuval don't make more of the irregularity than it deserves. Once they reissue the paper-

work on their end, I imagine our government will be fairly accommodating."

"You mean mine." Tanja shot a panicked look from Georgiou to Leon. "I'm taking Illi to Canada." Her tone brooked no argument.

As much as Leon had never wanted to be a father, the responsibility Tanja had thrust on him wasn't one he took lightly. It was onerous, but not in the way he had always expected it to be, which confounded him. In fact, the idea of leaving the full weight of Illi's future on Tanja felt downright wrong.

"They won't adopt her only to you. You need my name on there. For God's sake, Tanja. Look what I can offer her. Take advantage," he insisted.

She might have balked, but Georgiou set aside his notepad and folded his hands on the table, drawing a breath as if he had something important to say.

Georgiou had extricated Leon from several of the tight positions his father had left him in and had listened to the situation with Illi with equanimity, but looked very serious now.

"I agree with Leon. My advice is that you take no steps toward divorce until the adoption is airtight. What we could do is negotiate a postnuptial agreement. It's not much different from a prenup. Details will be negotiated with regards to support, division of property, and custody. That way, when the time comes, you can part amicably without any loose threads."

"Custody isn't up for negotiation." Fear of betrayal was lurking in Tanja's eyes as she looked up at Leon. And something else. A mistrust that he had earned.

The strangest clench wrapped around his lungs and squeezed, but he gave only a terse nod of agreement toward Georgiou. "Send a template. We'll start working things out."

Tanja looked like she wanted to argue, but Georgiou rose and flexed his back.

"Excellent." Georgiou grimaced. "And please forgive me, Leon, but my wife will kill me if I don't try to sell you a couple of tickets to her fundraiser next week. It's an auction of modern art to benefit a children's center in Athens."

"Of course," Leon said. Buying a couple of plates for charity was expected whether he showed up to eat whatever was served upon it or not. "Will it help for Tanja and I to circulate in public? With Illi's situation, I mean."

"It couldn't hurt. The more happily married you appear, the better."

"Oh, but—" Tanja started to protest.

"We'll be there," Leon confirmed, speaking over her. "Black tie?"

"White." Georgiou took out his phone. "I'll have her send the details, and I'll fetch Ester so we can finalize the press release." He slipped out, closing the door behind him.

"Hi. Remember me? Your wife?" Tanja asked tartly, rising to shake off her own tension. "I know you're new to this parenting gig, but I'm guessing children aren't invited to his wife's bake sale. What do you suggest we do with Illi? Leave her in the coat check?"

"Right. We need a nanny." He texted that to his PA.

"Leon." He glanced up to find Tanja's hands closed into fists, arms straight, chin lifted to a stubborn angle. "Illi has lost her entire family. Now she's lost Kahina and the only other people who were familiar to her. She has *me*. I refuse to shuffle her onto a nanny."

"I don't expect you to." He bit back pointing out Illi had him, too. "The gala will be in a hotel. She'll be upstairs asleep, not even missing you. Or playing with someone who is doting on her, same as she is right now." The crew members were determined to spoil her silly. "Wouldn't you prefer to have someone consistent sit with her when we have social obligations? We'll have several."

"How many is 'several'?" Her voice rose with panic. "I packed light for Istuval and packed even lighter when we left."

"The stylist will ensure you have everything you need." He pointed to the door, reminding her of the woman who'd come aboard with garment bags and makeup cases.

"She brought a handful of outfits for the photo shoot." Tanja flung out a hand.

"She'll arrange more," he said with equal exasperation. "It's her job to source your wardrobe. I presumed you understood that."

"What will *that* cost? I don't have a job, Leon!"

"I don't expect you to pay for it." Seriously, how was she not getting this? "I will."

"No."

He threw his head back, insulted all over again. "Why not?"

"I'm an *accountant*." She was red faced and strident, hands cutting through the air with agitation. "All the debits and credits have to balance or I can't sleep. I already feel like I'm in your debt for whatever Georgiou does on Illi's behalf."

"Quantify it, then," he shot back, losing patience. "Give me a number for the damage I did to your family. Deduct the value of your freedom and Illi's future well-being. When you have all of that calculated on a spreadsheet, we'll sit down and decide whether or not you can accept a damned sundress."

"But it's not *just* a sundress, is it?" she cried, not cowed in the least.

"No. It isn't," he agreed just as forcefully. "It's couture gowns and designer shoes. Jewelry. Spa visits if you want your toenails painted and handbags that go for five figures and are only big enough to carry a lipstick. I'm not telling you what to wear, Tanja, but you're my wife. These aren't gifts or bribes. These are the things you'll need in the life we'll be living. If we were going to the jungle, I'd buy you a mosquito net hat."

"But I'm *not* your wife!" She hugged herself defensively. "That's what I'm saying."

Something fierce welled in him, something he couldn't interpret and didn't want to. It made him want to throw aside the long table between them and pull her close.

"You are," he asserted, speaking reflexively and straight from the center of himself. "Until it's safe for

Illi that we divorce, you and I are married." He pointed at her. "And I'm going to do it right this time. I'll provide what you both need." That was not negotiable.

"So you expect me to just…" Her hand waved helplessly, and her brows came together with consternation. She bit her lip, tucking her hand under her elbow again, asking warily, "What *do* you expect?"

It struck him what she was asking and why she'd been so contrary for the last few minutes. It was a question that had been dancing around in his head while he avoided answering it himself. The way they were crossing swords right now told him the crackling heat between them wasn't going away. Hell, their midnight encounter had telegraphed that message loud and clear.

He drew a long drink of oxygen, trying to feed his lizard brain so it didn't take over and make him say or do something stupid. Somehow he had to remain civilized when what he wanted was purely instinctual.

"Given the way we both reacted last night," he said carefully, "I suggest we resume marital activities." His voice originated somewhere in the base of his chest, and heat detonated below his belt just thinking of what that might entail.

"Marital activities," she repeated in an astonished huff. A pink flush hit her cheeks, though. Pretty and shy and deeply aware.

Her flickering gaze was avoiding his, but he could see the latent sensations were teasing her, same as they were him. All he'd been thinking about since Illi interrupted them was that he wanted to crush Tanja close and celebrate her and *be inside* her.

"What do *you* expect?" he asked gruffly.

"I don't know what to expect from you!" Her anger resurfaced in a frustrated pang that caused a twist in his chest. "One minute you're so sweet with Illi and acting like a superhero, rescuing me and getting me a doctor. It makes me think I was right to be so enamored with you five years ago. Then you're ordering me to stay married and wear high heels to gala luncheons and resume having sex."

"I will *never* order you to have sex. Tell me you know that," he growled. "It's pretty damned insulting if you don't."

Her mouth quirked in concession. "I do, but you're still expecting a lot."

"Oh, like fatherhood?"

She stared flatly at him, refusing to engage on that one.

"Am I really expecting that much? It's dating, Tanja. Dinner and dancing and cocktail parties. Things we should have done rather than jump into marriage. What part of that bothers you? You've never been shy with strangers, so don't act like talking to people is a chore."

"I schmoozed my father's customers, asked them where they'd been and where they were going. That doesn't mean I know how to talk about history or modern art." She looked to her nails. "*You* didn't find me that interesting or you would have stuck around."

"Tanja."

"I don't want to be this insecure," she blurted, fist

punching the air beside her thigh again. "I don't want to go back to thinking I'm less than you are."

He snapped his head back. "Why did you ever? *You're not.*"

"I don't have this, Leon!" She threw her arm out to encompass the yacht. "I didn't have anything you wanted enough to bring you back to resume our marriage. The only thing I can give you now is a divorce and I can't even give you that! So what do I have that you want? Except..." Her wary, limpid eyes sent a sabre straight into his heart.

"Be very careful what you say next." He flattened his hands on the table, more incensed than he'd ever thought someone could make him. "Because sex has never been a transaction for me. I will not turn it into one with my *wife.*"

"What would it be then?" Her shoulders rose and fell, arms flailing helplessly. "Because we're only pretending we're married—"

"We *are* married."

"We're going to pretend that we're *staying* married and—"

"And act like any other couple who is married. Why not?"

"Because the only people I've ever slept with have been men I had feelings for. Men I thought had feelings for *me.*" She jabbed a finger at him. "And you don't."

CHAPTER SIX

LEON DIDN'T GET a chance to respond to that. There was a knock and Georgiou let himself in with his PR manager, Ester. Their amiable smiles died as they hit the wall of tension between her and Leon.

"Should we come back?" Ester asked, looking between them.

"No. We have to get the press release hammered out," Leon said grimly.

Tanja sat back down, body buzzing with adrenaline. With the idea of having sex with him. Was it what she wanted? Yes. On a strictly physical basis, she absolutely did want to finish what they'd started last night.

Emotionally, she didn't know if she could withhold enough of herself to walk away unscathed afterward. They called it "making love" for a reason. She knew herself well enough to know she would fall in love with him. She'd done what she could to dismiss and deny how badly he'd hurt her when he left, but she'd been crushed.

"Tanja?"

She was yanked out of her reverie by Leon's voice. His expression was inscrutable.

"Do you agree?"

Ugh. She'd completely missed everything that had been said and had to beg Ester to repeat it. A few minutes later, they had settled on a statement that she and Leon had married years ago in Canada. They had separated when he returned to Greece and recently reconciled. They were on a second honeymoon, enjoying the family they had started together.

The truth of how their daughter had come into their lives wasn't addressed. The announcement was very short on details, very tall on fairy-tale ending.

Tanja was put in a pretty wrap dress with a tropical print. Her hair was left loose and windswept while subtle makeup enhanced her features. They were photographed in casual settings around the yacht, some with Illi, some with just her and Leon.

They were standing against the rail in the bow, the sun setting behind them, when he touched her chin. She lifted her gaze, and all her turmoil got tangled up with the inscrutable emotions in his eyes.

As she read lust and remorse and something bright and fierce and possessive, her heart juddered to a stop in her chest. His thumb grazed her lips once, twice. Then he dipped his head and pressed the most tender kiss imaginable onto her mouth.

Last night's passion flared anew, blue with confusion in its center, but twisting a coiled flame of wistful longing and sparkling with the embers of dreams she'd believed were nothing but smoke and ash.

She curled her hand around his hard, flat wrist, losing herself to the sensation of his lips traveling over hers, turning a simple kiss into an exploration. A journey from regret to reconciliation.

How could a man kiss like this and feel none of the things that were swelling within her to the point of causing a deep, anguished ache?

His hand slid down to her neck and he slowly withdrew. Could he feel the way her pulse was pounding against the heel of his palm?

"That's beautiful," she heard from her right. She ducked her head. She'd forgotten they were under scrutiny and was mortified by all she must have let show nakedly on her face.

"That's enough," Leon said with an abrupt edge in his tone, cutting short the photography session with a jerk of his head.

When Tanja would have broken away from him, his arms hardened, keeping her in his embrace an extra second while he searched her expression. She set her hand on his chest and looked to the water, trying to compose herself.

But she felt his heart racing beneath the layers of muscle and bone, calling to her to stay close. Share in the tumult.

"Let's get them on their way," he said. "Then we can have a quiet dinner and talk."

It didn't work out that way. They had just said their goodbyes when Leon's mother texted. "I have to call her, prepare her for what to expect. You should touch base with your family. Let them know you'll be staying for the near future."

Before she could decide whether she wanted to protest his decree, Leon asked Kyle to fetch her a phone. Ten minutes later, she had unwrapped a brand-new smartphone, logged into her account and had her father on a video chat. It was so good to see him!

She didn't see Leon until she had put Illi down for the evening and was in the jet tub outside Leon's stateroom. He came out with a distracted, irritable look on his face.

"I hope you don't mind. Kyle found me a bathing suit." She self-consciously touched the halter strap of the neon pink bikini she wore, then pointed at the little device on the ledge. "And a baby monitor. He's like a genie. Why are you paying Georgiou to sort out our problems? Just ask Kyle to twitch his nose."

"Kyle's powers do not extend beyond the yacht." He began stripping down.

"What are you doing?" She snapped her head to the side, shielding her gaze.

"This tub is completely private. You don't need a suit. And it's been a long few days. I need to relax." His belt hit the deck with a faint, jangling thud. The rest of his clothes must have followed because he sank into the tub with a sigh of contentment. "Your Victorian aunt called. She wants her delicate sensibilities back."

"Ha-ha." Tanja couldn't tell if he was naked beneath the churning bubbles as she faced him across the small pool, but she would bet any money he was.

The side of his foot grazed her thigh when he propped his heels next to her hip and splayed out his long arms.

"What did your mother say?" she asked, trying not to be a prude by shifting away. She was actually the opposite—some kind of libertine who reacted to the brush of a foot like it was the most erotically provoking caress imaginable.

"You know how to kill a buzz, don't you?" His face hardened and his shoulders regained all their tension.

"Is that what she said?" she joked lamely.

He snorted, but there was little humor in it. "She wants us to come to dinner when we get to Athens. What did your father say?"

"That he wants me home," she said with a wrench of homesickness she couldn't keep from her voice. "He understands, though. He's ridiculously proud to have two grandchildren." She smiled as she recalled her father's button-busting enthusiasm. He was also worried that Leon would hurt her or let her down again. So was she, but she kept that to herself.

"My mother didn't say any of that," Leon said flatly, cheekbones like calved glaciers they were so sharp and ghostly blue in the glow from beneath the surface of the water.

Tanja started to point out that Illi wasn't his so why would his mother welcome her as a grandchild, but the mood he was radiating didn't seem receptive to hearing excuses for his mother's behavior.

"When you said your parents' marriage was horrific, what did you mean?"

His breath left him in a disparaging exhale. "Name it. They both cheated. Used me against one another. Had ugly fights where they threw things and humiliated each other in public."

"That's awful. Were there drug or alcohol issues?"

"They didn't admit to it or seek help, so is that a valid excuse?" His arm bent and he used his thumbnail to scratch his eyebrow. "My father was a terrible person. Profoundly selfish and manipulative. My mother brought her own father's money into the marriage and would have divorced him if he would have given it back, but he refused. In fact, he hired a man to seduce her and take intimate photos, then held them as blackmail over her. I think I've got all the copies destroyed by now, but who knows? He could still haunt her with them."

"That's horrible!"

"It is. She was pretty horrible sometimes, too. I've had three DNA tests to prove I'm his. Frankly, I was hoping every time I wouldn't be. When I was eight, he sent me to boarding school purely to punish her. Sometimes I think I should have tried harder to refuse."

"You were eight. How much choice did you have?"

"None, but I knew she was upset. We had a decent relationship until then. It was damaged beyond repair after I left, and a lot of that is on me. She quit showing affection for me, though, so he wouldn't keep using me against her. It made it hard to tell if she wanted me to... I don't know. Fight to see her? I was just happy to be away from all of it so I took every excuse to avoid going home. That's how I got into racing. I crewed through school breaks and bought my first sailboat by saving up my allowance." His mouth twisted with self-mockery. He knew how spoon-fed that sounded.

"Did your mother know your father wasn't always operating within the law?"

"She had suspicions," he said with weariness. "She was afraid to ask too many questions." He was deep in thought, absently working his thumb against his bent finger. "When I came home for the funeral and we began to realize how bad things were, she cried for the first time I'd seen in years. She said, 'I hung on through all of that so you would inherit, and now there's nothing?' It was a kick in the gut to realize she thought she had been helping me by staying with him."

"So you rebuilt your father's fortune for *her*?"

His gaze flickered to hers, eyes flinty slits. "And the thousands of people around the globe who needed their jobs."

Right.

"Does she feel threatened by me? Not me specifically, but the fact you have a wife?"

He let his head drop back against the edge of the tub again. "She's angry I never told her I was married."

"Ever?"

"We aren't close," he said flatly.

Tanja slouched deeper into the water to absorb that, absently bringing her feet up to the edge of the bench across from her. She jerked away when her foot touched Leon's firm thigh.

His hand slid beneath the surface and caught her ankle, bringing it back, holding her gaze as he set her foot in place on the bench next to his hip before his arm returned to the edge of the tub.

The heat and churn and burble of the water filled the air. It was a manifestation of the conflicting energy between them. Of the clear head she was trying to keep while, below the surface, her body was roiling with sensations. Her heart was doing somersaults, trying to take in how Leon's childhood had turned him into a man who had been charming, yet withdrawn. One who inspired confidence, then ultimately let her down.

"I wouldn't stay with a man who treated me like that," she told him quietly, meaning it, but also aware that his brief touch had left her simmering in more than the warmth of the water. Yearning was sitting in the pit of her stomach.

"Not even for Illi? Because you weren't *eating*, Tanja."

"I ate." Not enough, but she understood. "You're right, though. I don't know what lengths I would go to for my child, but I have the luxury of family and friends who I know would support me, which gives me options. Obviously, your mother didn't feel like she had any."

"I hate that I'm not on that list. That I had to hear through your brother that you needed help," he muttered. "I'm not proud of the way I left you. Or the circumstances I left you in. It's the kind of thing my father would have done. Waiting for you to come to me to resolve things was just like him, too. The fact you never did, that you had too much self-respect to make the first move..." His dark brows lowered with intensity. "Don't ever think you're less than me. You have far more integrity than I ever will. Than most people I know."

"That is an extremely generous thing to say, given the position I've put you in with Illi," she pointed out, both touched and contrite.

"You wouldn't have had to do that, wouldn't have gone to Istuval or wound up so broke you were going hungry, if I'd looked after you properly. I'm going to make that up to you with the postnuptial."

"I don't want your money, Leon."

"I know. But it's important to me that I do this right this time. My opening offer is a million euros per year of marriage."

"That's ridiculous! *No*," she insisted.

"And every time you say something like that—" he tipped his head back, speaking to the starry sky "—I'm going to double it."

She held back a reflexive protest, hesitated, then asked, "Don't you mean halve it?"

"No." His head came up. "Another woman might play those games, trying to up the amount, but you won't."

He said it confidently, as if he *knew* her. That seeming approval and admiration increased all the sweet tugs and pulls in her middle and provoked her into teasing him.

"What happens if I ask you to double it?"

"Done."

"Leon! Don't you dare."

"You understand that when it doubles again, we're going from two to four?" He tilted his face to the sky again, and she thought he might be laughing at her.

"Will you please be serious?" she asked, heart pounding with genuine alarm.

"I'm completely serious. I know you don't want my money." His humor was gone, his voice dispassionate. "You've said it several times already. But I need the amount to be attractive enough that you'll leave if things get bad. *Before* they get bad. I need to know that I won't spend my entire life causing damage to another human being. That Illi won't be caught in the cross fire. I want us both to have a clean exit if things are unbearable."

"Would it be, though?"

He picked up his head.

"Do whatever you want with your money. I don't care, but—" She hesitated, then spoke her greatest fear aloud. "I'm afraid that if I sleep with you, I'll fall in love with you." Again. She didn't admit that last bit because she'd lost her ability to breathe. She felt as though her lungs were locked, no air getting into them.

"Have you been listening? I'm not worth your love." His jaw was clenched, his mouth tense, his biceps like smooth, tanned rocks.

"Your father was not a good person. It doesn't mean you aren't."

"I need you to stay realistic, Tanja." He spoke softly, but it didn't leech any of the power from his words. "I am capable of charm and consideration, but I'm not capable of love. Don't mistake my desire to be good to you for actual goodness within me. Don't mistake my desire for you as anything more than intense sexual attraction."

Her heart was being stretched in all directions by his words, until it was thin and threatening to unravel completely.

"But I do want you," he said thickly, making her heart lurch and stumble into a gallop. A tic appeared in his cheek. "Other women won't do. I want *you*. I want that fire we tasted last night. I made myself forget how uniquely well suited we are, but there's no denying it. And I can't *stand* the idea of not experiencing it again."

The backs of her eyes were hot. So was her throat. Her mind was reeling, trying to reason through all the warnings he'd just voiced that he couldn't be entrusted with her heart.

Ironically, his stark honesty made her trust him a little. Maybe she was only rationalizing what she really wanted, though. Because she wanted the fire, too. She couldn't imagine living her life alongside him, calling herself his wife, and not allowing their combined conflagration to engulf her.

Before she let herself think it through any further, she nodded. "Okay."

For two heartbeats, time stopped.

Then he moved like a shark. Like a sea monster. Like Poseidon himself as he scooped her up in the same motion of standing and rising from the tub. Water sluiced off them while she clung to him in shock.

He strode without ceremony into the bedroom and set her on the bed.

"We're wet—"

He was already coming down on top of her, naked and still dripping, body burning with heat from the water. Their skin was abraded with damp friction as he pushed a knee between hers and spread her legs so he could settle between them. His mouth came down over hers, smothering her. Ravaging her. Consuming her.

They were instantly in the center of the storm, where they'd been last night, but even deeper in the maelstrom. She jammed her fingers into his hair and angled her head so the seal of their mouths deepened. His tongue thrust in and she moaned as she greeted his intrusion.

His weight was a glorious pressure pinning her to the mattress while the steely length of his naked shaft sat firm and undeterred by the wet triangle of fabric between her thighs.

He lifted his head abruptly and drew the tied strap from behind her neck over her head, dragging it down to reveal her breasts, the pale orbs topped by nipples drawn tight as the warm night air hit them. One hot hand cupped her clammy breast, making her writhe at the conflicting sensations. His gaze dragged upward even as he toyed with the hard button.

"Your hair. Your skin," he said in a gritty voice, as though words were failing him. Or he wanted to use his mouth for too many things. His lips traversed from her cheek to her neck and back up to nip her jaw, then into her neck again, hot tongue sweeping into the hollow beneath her ear. "I want to lick every inch of you."

She wanted that, too. Everything. All of him. Fast. Her hands were moving over his flexing shoulders, the sweep of her touch drying him. Her legs climbed to hug his waist tight. As she lifted her hips into his erection, she breathed his name like a mantra. "Leon. Leon."

"Every inch, Tanja. Every damned inch," he muttered, trailing his kisses down her arm to the inside of her elbow before he crossed her arm over her chest, lifting and shifting as he rolled her onto her stomach beneath him.

He tugged at the tie on her top and yanked her bottoms down before his naked weight settled on her again. The steely heat of his shaft nestled in the crease of her damp buttocks and a cloud of humid, gratified breath touched the side of her face, telling her he needed this as badly as she did. She could feel his heart slamming into her back, could hear him swallow and pant another shaken breath against her shoulder.

Despite those signs of tenuous control, his fingers traced a deliberate, tickling line across the tops of her shoulders, skimming the wet tails of her hair away before he kissed the top of her spine.

She gasped, arching as his benediction sent a shiver to her lower back. He set about nuzzling her nape and the back of her shoulder, her ear and the back of her arm. He was braced on one elbow, using his free hand to caress from her waist to her ribs, causing her skin to tighten all over her body.

She was nearly helpless, dominated this way, but she lifted her backside to caress him, moaning to let him know how much she needed this—to be worshipped as he conquered her. Caressed and teased and adored.

His open mouth zigzagged across her back and he drew one of her knees up so she was exposed to his touch when his fingers sought the fine curls that protected her damp, intimate folds.

They both took shaken inhales as he found the honeyed sweetness there. He was barely touching her, but her flesh was so swollen and wanton, it only took the lightest of explorations to make her shiver and moan into the pillow.

"Good?"

"Yes. But I need more," she begged, barely able to speak. Her hands clawed into the blankets beneath her and she moved her hips, seeking his touch, rubbing her face into the pillow. "Touch inside me."

"Soon," he said in a rasp against her lower back. He set his teeth against one cheek in a playful bite, before he rose and rolled her onto her back again.

She was losing all inhibition. Her legs fell open so

he had room between them, bikini bottoms dislodged so they sat across her mound. She stared boldly into his face as he loomed over her, waiting for his gaze to come back after he dragged her top free and threw it off the side of the bed. He ate up what he had exposed, his fierce expression terrifying in its intensity.

Yet she exalted in it. In being *his*.

Her breasts were swollen with anticipation. Her nipples drawn tight by the chill and arousal. With a growl, he dropped his head to close his searing mouth over her nipple and pulled so strongly, bright spears of sensation went straight into her loins.

"Leon," she cried, squirming at the intensity.

"Bear it," he commanded, and looped one arm behind her waist, arching her as he moved to the other breast to suck and tease.

She was losing her mind to pure carnality, ready to do anything at his command. She pulled at his hair, insisting, "Kiss me."

"I will," he said, prying her fingers from his thick curls and biting the heel of her hand before he slid down and rained kisses on her ribs, her stomach, her jutting hipbones.

She was trembling, shaking with anticipation. Weak.

He set the softest, sweetest kiss on her inner thigh. She nearly screamed.

"What's wrong, beautiful?" he teased. But as he looked up at her, the lust in his gaze hit her like a punch.

Her breath left her so quickly she was dizzy, and

the heat flooding her loins redoubled. The ache there intensified as he took his sweet time playing his tongue into the crease of her knee and along her calf, biting her instep, making her wait and wait and wait.

When he caught his hands in her suit, dragging it off her hips and down her legs, she lifted to help.

Naked, she gave a slow thrash against the covers, all of her so completely afire by his hot gaze roaming over her, she barely felt the wet patches beneath her.

With one hand, he held his length in a restrictive fist. His other caressed her calf to her thigh to the crease of her hip, spreading her legs wider, gaze unabashedly drinking her in.

Her stomach quivered in nervous reaction. She glanced at the windows surrounding them, noted the doors to the deck and jet tub were still wide open.

"Someone might see us," she gasped.

"No one will come. Except you." He set a smile that turned into a kiss against her inner knee. "And me." He kissed his way up to her mound.

She spoke his name on a sob. A plea.

"I missed this." His touch parted her and his tongue swept through her folds, making her whole body jerk at the streak of lightning that shot through her. He made a reassuring noise and set a steadying hand on her stomach. "Tell me hard or soft," he murmured, curling his other arm around her thigh as he began to make love to her with his mouth.

She could only groan helplessly. Her hand tangled in his hair while wet heat built. Her thighs closed of their own accord, the ministrations of his mouth causing sensations so intense they were nearly unbearable.

She had missed this, too. So much. When he ignored her plea that he fill her, she abandoned herself to the pleasure he was determined to bestow. She gave in to the quivering tension building in her stomach. Abandoned herself to the growing waves of keening joy.

Suddenly a shuddering climax had her lifting her hips and muffling her cries with the back of her wrist. It was so good she could have wept.

Was he arrogant in his triumph when he rose over her? Hell, yes. He looked her over from hairline to the soles of her feet, missing none of the trembling, vanquished aftermath he had caused.

Did she care that he wore barbaric satisfaction like an aura? Not one iota. She was too sated. Yet empty. Yearning.

"Do I need a condom?" His voice was such a deep growl it might have originated from the middle of the earth. Like an element. Iron. Or gold.

She nodded jerkily.

He sent her a look of amused mock terror as he reached into the nightstand. "There better be one in here."

There was. Seconds later, he settled over her and they both sighed at the press of their damp skin, like the sizzle on a hotplate.

And even though she was dying for him to thrust into her, he kissed her until she was lifting her hips against his hardness again. Inviting him.

He lightly bit her earlobe and said, "Tell me how much." The wide crest of his tip pressed against her sensitized flesh, stretching her with a pinch she hadn't realized she'd missed. It stung a little, but she arched to make it easy for him. He sank all the way in with one slow, inexorable thrust, until they were meshed to the depths of their flesh and she could feel his very heartbeat within her.

She could have died then, her sense of fulfilment was so complete.

They kissed, unmoving, his restraint making him shake as he passionately devoured her mouth. Sweet curls of renewed desire grew in coils of increasing tension, prompting her to wrap her arms and legs around him, wanting him deeper. Wanting to stay like this, linked and still. Indelible.

Eventually he shifted, and the small movement awakened her to the exquisite pleasures awaiting both of them.

"This," she groaned under his first lazy thrusts. She scraped her hands from his hair to his neck to his shoulders, down to his lower back and up again, trying to feel all of him at once.

His guttural noise agreed with her. He held himself on one elbow, his hand hooked beneath her shoulder so he could thrust with more power. He watched her with glittering eyes as she gloried in his lovemaking.

She welcomed each gentle slam of his hips, moaning with encouragement when he came back with more strength. She had forgotten this. Or hadn't let herself remember how utterly overwhelming their lovemaking was. Nothing existed but the sharp lines of his face, the pierce of pleasure that went through her with each stroke of his body into hers. Intense yearning held her still for each return, so the reverberations of pleasure spun out to sting her fingertips and toes.

They were both making animalistic noises, holding back nothing. Hiding nothing. That was the part that made their lovemaking so tremendous and devastating at once. They were watching the other, unable to hide their need, their craving, their rejoicing.

That honesty was too much. She knew her surrender would be written large, too. She couldn't bear it, yet she couldn't resist it. The tension between those imperatives couldn't be sustained.

Her nails dug into his shoulders. His fingertips bit into her hip. She clenched her teeth, trying to hold back, trying to maintain her slippery grip on this plateau of incredible connection. His face contorted with his struggle. He quickened his pace.

"Come," he commanded in a jagged voice. "Come with me. Do it now."

She gave in to the abyss. Pleasure detonated within her, sending her spinning in all directions while he slid his arms under her and bucked heavily into her. His head went back and his neck strained as he shouted his release.

CHAPTER SEVEN

HOW HAD HE left that? That was Leon's first rational thought when he discarded the condom and flopped back onto the bed beside Tanja, completely spent.

His next thought was, *It's still too much*. He was so raw his chest felt torn open.

Yet, as the breeze danced across their cooling bodies, he couldn't make himself do anything but drag her close and tuck her head under his chin. The boneless lassitude in her heavy limbs and the satiated sigh that warmed his collarbone eased something in him.

"Did we wake Illi?" she asked with tremulous humor.

"She'd let us know if she was awake." The kid wasn't afraid to use the full capacity of her lungs if she decided to lodge a complaint. When he'd taken her out of the swing this morning, she'd publicly denounced him for human rights violations.

"That was really good." Tanja kissed his throat, skimming a light touch from his shoulder to his neck, but he felt the shaking that lingered in her. "Thank you."

That tiny betrayal of how deeply she'd been affected shook things loose inside him.

He wanted to pry at least a mental space between them since he couldn't make himself do it physically, but he had to say, "Thank *you*," because this had been better than good. It had been incredible.

He wished he could blame his powerful release on breaking his celibacy, but he knew it was more than that. He didn't understand how one woman could strip him down to such an elemental place. Tanja wasn't particularly unique. He'd met many women who were easy on the eye, smart and funny, tolerant yet assertive. Ones who liked sex as much as he did. Before he'd married, he'd made love with those other women and always enjoyed it, but he had never felt this same deconstruction of his inner self after the fact.

He'd like to think it was only happening because he had changed from the man he'd been, but if anything, he was more guarded, not less. And Tanja had affected him this way before he'd lost his father and left her. He remembered this same postcoital sensation of exposure that warned his defenses were down.

Was *this* why he'd left her and not looked back?

It was a disturbing thought. He didn't want to see himself as a child who ran away from something because it was uncomfortable, but that's exactly the coping strategy he'd employed for his early years. It had been disguised as school exams and regatta trials and whatever pursuits he could conjure as an excuse. It had been an avoidance tactic to escape his troubled home life and the toll it took upon him, plain and simple.

Since his father's death, he'd learned to face his problems head-on, though, and did.

But how could he face and resolve this? He could barely articulate the issue. Tanja wasn't purposely chipping away at his soul. He was opening up despite every instinct in him warning against it. It went far beyond physical. He had few inhibitions there, but he had revealed things to her about his father and his childhood, things he'd never told anyone. They were the sorts of things that could be used as weapons the way his parents had used their own weaknesses against each other.

He almost wished Tanja had told him to go to hell when he had made his case for them to resume having sex.

I'm afraid that if I sleep with you, I'll fall in love with you.

He was afraid she would, too. He couldn't lead her on again, but he couldn't dodge, run or otherwise distance himself. That would be cowardly.

The fact was that he wanted to be right where he was, able to put his hands on her as freely as he liked. Drinking in her scent and combing his fingers through the fine strands of her hair as she relaxed with a soft murmur against him.

With a sudden inhale of realization, she tilted her head back. "What if I never claim it?"

"What?"

"The settlement." A gotcha smile danced around

her mouth. "If we never divorce, then I never have to accept your money. I've got you, haven't I?"

Whatever came into his features caused her expression to flinch and fall into stiff lines.

"It was a joke," she said with a note of hurt.

"I know. It's fine," he lied, tucking her face under his chin again, heart unsteady. He was barely able to pick apart the intense emotions that were throbbing like live nerve endings throughout his body. He had sudden visions of the arrows his parents had refused to cease aiming at one another, only this time they were aimed at Tanja.

No.

"I grew up with a brother," she was muttering. "I learned to be competitive. I wanted to prove I could outsmart you, that's all." The trusting way she'd been relaxed against him had evaporated. She was nothing but bony, ropy tension now.

"I know," he assured her with a single sweep of his palm down her narrow back. But he'd heard more beneath her remark than excitement at finding a loophole. He might not know everything about his wife, but he knew she believed in people and futures and family. "But do you remember what I said about being realistic?" he asked gently.

She was silent for a long time, but the way she was holding her breath told him she was still awake. Hell, she wasn't fighting tears, was she? That would kill him.

When she spoke, her voice held the toughness he'd

always admired in her. "I think you underestimate my desire to win," she said with quiet dignity.

And she was underestimating his willingness to lose, especially if it meant she and her child would be better off in the long run. He only kissed her forehead and said, "Let's just enjoy what we have right now."

Tanja woke in a lingering stupor from their love-making. Leon had risen in the night to close all the doors. Within moments of him returning to the bed, they'd been making love again with equally cataclysmic results.

That had been deeply reassuring, given how he'd reacted to her suggestion they stay married. She hadn't meant to sound so... Ugh. She threw her arm over her eyes, angry with herself over something that had been a stupid joke.

One that had brimmed with wistful yearning on her part, she had realized once he'd brutally shut down "forever" as an option. Recalling his "be realistic" warning—*twice*—caused sharp cracks to fracture from the middle of her heart outward, making all her bones ache.

Tanja was a hopeful person by nature. She couldn't help thinking they had something, given that neither of them had slept with anyone else in five years. Their first time falling into bed again had probably registered on nearby seismographs.

But things were happening much as they had the last time. Leon turned her head. Of course he did. He was a man who had everything—looks and wit and smarts. Wealth and confidence and, as it turned out, a massive soft spot for a baby who wasn't even his.

Any woman in the world would find him irresistible and spin a few fantasies about hitching her future to his.

Tanja had opened her heart to him once already, though. And look what happened. He'd walked away and five years had passed without a word. He had only come to her in Istuval because he'd thought doing her a favor would make their divorce go more smoothly.

He *wanted* a divorce. She had to remember that. Leon might want her body, but he didn't want to make a life with her and her daughter. When all this was over, would he even keep up a relationship with Illi? If Tanja was being realistic, she had to go on the assumption she and Leon would part ways permanently this time.

Oh, that hurt. It felt like failure, which was silly. Her future would still hold Illi and, hopefully, Brahim. It would be a very rich life. She didn't need a man to complete it. She and Leon had never stood a real chance anyway. That's what she was learning.

Surely they could be friends, though? She "liked" the photos of her first love's baby and supported her high school boyfriend's music ambitions by downloading his songs. She and Leon were sharing intensely personal things, their bodies among them. Did all of that mean nothing to him? Would he really be able to walk away and forget her completely?

As she stared at the ceiling, heart aching, she had

to reconcile herself to the fact she might, indeed, mean very little to him. He was a closed-off, compartmentalized type of man.

"Well, that's quite an opinion," she heard Leon say, which made a spike of awareness flash through her, as though he'd read her thoughts, but he was talking to Illi, quiet and indulgent. "I've had executives on my payroll who don't make as much sense as you do. Try to keep it down, though. Mommy is still sleeping."

Tanja realized the distant, garbled squawks she kept hearing weren't a seabird.

"I'm awake," she called.

A pause, then Leon brought Illi in. She was chewing her fist and wearing a fresh onesie.

Leon, the scoundrel, wore nothing but a pair of low-slung boxers and undiluted sex appeal. The sight of his strong arm curled so securely around her daughter lit up all of Tanja's biological buttons. *Love her. Love us both*, she wanted to beg him.

He set Illi on the rumpled blankets next to her. His expression was shuttered, but his lashes flickered as though his gaze saw through the covers and tracked restlessly over her naked skin.

"Her bottle is on the way. So is breakfast. I have to make some calls, but we'll take the helicopter to Athens as soon as we're ready."

"Oh." Reality. She was starting to hate it. Why couldn't they float along in this honeymoon-like bubble aboard the yacht?

His gaze finally hit hers, tangling up with the conflicted yearning twisting in her gut. His was mostly unreadable, but she saw the memories there of their torrid night, the flash of hunger in the way he stopped himself from swooping down over her like a hawk.

Before she realized what she was doing, she lifted her arm in invitation.

He dug his knee into the mattress and leaned across Illi's small, kicking body. The weight of his mouth pressed Tanja onto her back while she received the most tender ravishment imaginable.

She moaned in a mix of startled reaction and shaken nerves. She hadn't expected him to drag her so easily into the miasma of need for his mouth, his touch. She was distantly aware of Illi squirming beneath the bridge of his body, but each time he started to draw away, Tanja pressed her fingertips into the back of his neck and he came back. He delved and tasted, and left her hot and dazed and utterly breathless.

Finally, he disobeyed her urging and lifted away.

He remained braced over the two of them, his one hand on Tanja's far side, his gaze tracking over what had to be a very flushed and dazzled expression on her face.

"Temptress." It was more accusation than compliment, but his mouth twisted in self-deprecating humor. "Ogling me like I'm ice cream on a hot summer's day."

She folded her wet, swollen lips together and lifted the sheet enough to peek beneath, deliberately teasing him because, when they were like this, they were perfectly aligned.

"So I am." She sealed the edge across her breasts and pinned the sheet with her arm. "Too bad I can't show you. I'm definitely in the mood for ice cream. Not plain vanilla, either."

His gaze warmed with amusement and remained locked with hers as he eased back. He touched Illi's fine hair on his way. As he straightened to stand beside the bed, he spoke in a voice that was more threat or command than the imparting of information.

"The nanny interviews start today."

Interlude of flirtation aside, Tanja climbed aboard the helicopter with reservations.

The romantic in her wanted to believe she was embarking on a chance to see if her marriage *could* work. She'd never been someone who did anything by half measures so she instinctually wanted to give their union a real chance, but beneath Leon's hot kiss and patience while she ran around looking for that one worn T-shirt she didn't need but didn't want to lose, she felt the inner walls he was erecting against her.

It hurt and made for a disheartening start to a difficult flight. Leon sat as copilot and Illi cried the whole way. Tanja was frazzled by the time they landed on Leon's rooftop penthouse in Athens. Leon's PA, Demitri, met them and showed Tanja to a spare bedroom that had quickly been converted into a nursery for Illi.

"Decorators will arrive today to take measurements and discuss color schemes, but I hope it suffices for the moment?" Demitri asked anxiously.

Illi had never had a real crib or change table, let alone a surplus of supplies, clothes and toys.

"It's perfect," Tanja assured him, relieved to have somewhere to safely put Illi down since she had worn herself out on the flight and her eyelids were already drooping.

Tanja tucked her in and carried the baby monitor as she explored the airy living space.

Much like the yacht, everything was modern and bright and reflective of understated yet undeniable luxury. Beyond the wall of windows, Leon was sitting down with Georgiou at the courtyard dining table next to the infinity pool. Was that the Acropolis in the distance? It was so close it looked like she could swim to the edge of the water and reach out to touch it.

A middle-aged woman in the kitchen was making coffee and preparing platters filled with dips and bread sticks, olives and cheese, stuffed vine leaves and grilled octopus. She introduced herself as the housekeeper and chef, Valerie.

Huh. No wonder Leon had never felt a need for his wife to join him.

"I was hoping for a drink of water," Tanja said, glancing around for a glass.

"Sparkling or still?"

"Tap water is fine."

"I have this cucumber water to go with the meze?" Valerie brought a jug from the refrigerator.

"Um, sure. Thank you."

It was the same over-the-top level of service Tanja had experienced on the yacht, and it began to hit her that the yacht was not an exception. This was how Leon lived. He had lived like this all his life. It was disconcerting, making her feel as though she'd been transported into a movie or some other surreal world.

She would have loved a moment to catch her breath and process it, but she only had time to grab a bite with the men before a parade of appointments tied her up.

Her stylist from the yacht arrived and brought her into the other spare bedroom, now filled with racks of clothing. "We don't have to go through all of this right now, but I wanted to pick out a few key pieces so I can alter them if they need it."

Tanja was measured and pinned and soon turned out in a blue-and-white-striped sundress that she adored on sight—it buttoned down the front and had big patch pockets. But she had no time to browse the rest of the clothes. The health nurse arrived.

Tanja assured the woman she was recovering nicely but was given iron pills, and the chef was instructed on her nutritional needs.

The nurse left and Tanja was promptly served a protein smoothie and dense cookies filled with dates and nuts. Then the potential nanny arrived. Leon surprised her by joining her. He asked questions Tanja wouldn't have thought to ask, like how flexible the young woman was to travel and, "Can you start tonight?"

"I brought a bag in case you needed me right now," Britta said with a warm smile.

"Excellent." Leon looked to Tanja as she snapped a glare at him. "What? You'll be tied up getting ready."

"For what?" she asked with beleaguered panic.

"Dinner with my mother."

"That's *tonight*? I thought—" She didn't know what she had thought. She sagged into the sofa, stricken at how quickly things were spinning beyond her control.

"Will you take these to the kitchen, please?" Leon nodded at the empty dishes, dismissing the nanny. "Don't look so anxious," he chided Tanja. "Mother's apartment is two floors down."

"Then why don't we bring Illi? Doesn't she want to meet her?"

Something hardened in Leon's expression. "Let the nanny get her feet wet. This will ease you into trusting her, if you know you can come back up if it's not working."

True. She sighed her agreement, saying absently, "I didn't realize your mother owns an apartment in this building, too." It seemed odd that she hadn't come up to greet them. Had Leon invited her?

"I own the building," he said very casually, as though it was a totally normal thing for a person to say. "My mother prefers the island and travels a lot, but she stays here when she's in Athens. Tell the stylist semiformal for dinner. I'll shower and change into a suit."

Tanja's heart lurched again as his outrageous level of wealth hit her. No wonder he had assumed she'd married him for his money. What a bumpkin he must have thought her with her sundress from the farmers market and her discount sandals.

She heard Illi on the monitor and fetched her to introduce her to Britta. They warmed to each other immediately, which was reassuring.

Tanja had to put her trust in the stylist as much as the nanny, accepting the silver-blue satin dress she picked out. It was deceptively simple with a deep V-neck and sleeves that went to her elbows. The bodice hugged her braless breasts and a wide band accentuated her narrow waist. The skirt was a voluminous A-line that ended midshin, perfectly showcasing a flashy shoe with crystal-encrusted heels. Thankfully, they were closed toe, because she was desperately in need of a pedicure.

"Tomorrow," her stylist promised her, sweeping Tanja's hair off one ear with a spangled clip.

Tanja nervously joined Leon in the lounge. It struck her that they'd never been on a proper date. They'd gone out on his yacht, and eaten barbecue with her family, picked up lunch for a hike, but they'd never put on their best clothes and gone out in public.

"I feel overdressed for dinner," she murmured to announce her presence.

He turned and stood arrested with a glass halfway to his mouth. After his gaze went to her ankles and came back, he finished his drink in one gulp.

"You look perfect. This is for you, too." He picked up a velvet ring box off a side table and brought it to her.

"That's not necessary. I have my wedding band,"

she stammered, glancing toward the bedrooms. "It's in my bag. I was going to trade it for groceries at one point, but—"

"You should have." His jaw hardened. "Why didn't you?"

"I wasn't sure of the protocol," she said with a humorless chuckle. "Like, I know you're supposed to return the engagement ring if you're the one who calls it off, but are you supposed to give back the wedding band if you ask for a divorce?"

"I don't know, but they're both gifts. Do what you like with them." He spoke firmly. "Sell this one tomorrow if you want to." He opened the box and her knees grew weak.

This was not the simple gold wedding band she had worn for a few months, then yanked off in a fit of pique. This was a platinum band with five emerald-cut diamonds set in a glittering row. It had to be worth five figures, maybe six.

"Leon," she said in a muted beg for understanding. "I can't."

"Can't what? Wear it or not. It's yours." He was speaking so abruptly, each word hit like little pebbles against her skin. "Or exchange it for something you like better."

"Of course, I *like* it. It's stunning. But…" She frowned with consternation, trying to make him see that wearing his ring *meant* something. Didn't it? "Is wearing it like wearing this?" She fluffed the fall of her skirt, and even that small action felt like blowing air against a scraped knee. "Part of the costume?"

His head jerked back.

"Because—" She was struggling to find words that wouldn't reveal how much she was tripping over her own insecurity and involuntary expectations. "I mean, I'll wear it if you want me to, so people don't ask awkward questions, but it's important to me that you know I don't expect any of this. I'm not here for dresses and jewelry." And all those other things he insisted he wanted to give her because she was his wife.

Was he compensating because he wasn't capable of offering himself? That struck her as heartbreakingly sad for both of them.

"I know why you're here." His voice held an edge. "If I could make Illi yours as easily as I can provide a dress or a ring, I would. For now, this is how we make that happen."

By playing the happy couple.

That's all this ring was. Window dressing. A means to an end.

With an ache behind her sternum, she put it on.

The ring looked a bit loose, but Tanja needed to gain a few pounds. It would fit perfectly in a few weeks. Would she still be here then?

Leon refused to think about that.

It bothered him that she'd been so reluctant to accept it even though he'd been perfectly honest in saying he didn't care what she did with it. Okay, that was a small lie. He damned well *expected* her to sell it for food or anything else she might need if she was ever in dire straits again—not that he intended to let that happen.

He'd given the ring to her for her future security and because his mother would expect his wife to wear a ring of a certain quality. He told himself he wasn't attached to either ring or wife beyond recognizing they each held their own type of value and deserved his protection.

But he was inexplicably pleased to see the diamonds flash on her hand as they entered the elevator. He looked into the mirrored wall that reflected infinite versions of his pale gray suit and her silver-blue dress. Her fiery hair and cinnamon freckles stood out like sparking flames. A swell of pride filled him.

"You look stunning."

She relaxed into a natural smile for the first time since this morning and might have turned into his arms if the elevator hadn't stopped with a muted ping.

For half a moment, he'd forgotten where they were going. Now a clammy blanket descended on him. His mother. If he could have kept Tanja away from this, he would have. It was his greatest shame that he didn't come from a family like hers. If there was a silver lining to bringing her here now, it was that she would never have to meet his father—this would be excruciating enough. His mother would be...

Well, she would hurt Tanja without even trying. Because that's what she did.

Tanja's expression fell into the stoic one that had overtaken his own face. He clasped her hand and guided her down the hall to double doors that let into his mother's foyer.

His mother's living space was laid out much as his own, but there were two units on this floor, so hers was smaller with only two bedrooms and didn't have a pool. His mother had a more feminine decor and classic art pieces of fruit bowls and landscapes rather than the modern abstracts he preferred.

Truthfully, Leon gravitated to whatever was the opposite of what he'd grown up with.

"Leon." His mother guarded her appearance scrupulously. She was trim and should have developed more frown and worry lines, given how intimidated and angry she'd been for many of her sixty-two years. She wore a silk coat dress with a popped collar and broke from a small group of equally well-dressed guests to approach them.

Leon grimly surveyed the number of people she'd invited. He had thought they'd been invited for dinner, not a dinner *party*.

Tanja's hand tightened in his. Maybe she was reacting to his own firming grip. As his mother approached, his hackles rose out of instinctive protectiveness.

Tanja smiled with her natural appealing openness even as her gaze flickered to the crowd that was staring. Her smile barely faltered, though.

"Mother, my wife Tanja. Tanja, my mother, Ophelia."

"It's lovely to meet you." Tanja dropped his hand and automatically extended her arms for an embrace.

Of course, she did. That's how she was with family, and his mother was now a member.

His stomach cramped as Ophelia neatly caught her hands and pressed them down into the space between them. She kept her arms straight and firm, holding Tanja off from closing the distance. Her smile tightened.

Tanja took it as the rebuff it was. Leon knew she did because he saw the flinch that she quickly stifled, reinvigorating her smile to hide it.

He mentally willed an invisible, bulletproof box to lower itself over her to keep her from the death by a thousand cuts that had shredded him his whole life.

"It's lovely to meet you, too, after all this time," his mother was saying, almost sounding sincere despite the way she had scorned Tanja's warmth. "Welcome to the family. Ah, Cornelius." She let go of Tanja and twined her hands around the arm of a heavyset older man Leon had met a few times. They exchanged nods. "Cornelius, this is my daughter-in-law, Tanja. Come. Let us introduce you to everyone."

They made the rounds. Leon stayed close, but Tanja quickly began to look less like herself. Her smiles became forced. Her cheeks grew pale, her responses careful. Was she feeling sick again? Or was she hating this as much as he was?

"Did I hear you're a model, Tanja?" someone asked.

"A CPA. In Canada, that stands for chartered professional accountant," she explained to all the faces that went blank. "I articled at a firm that serves hotels and other tourism-related businesses on Vancouver Island."

A man laughed, then abruptly sobered. "Oh, you're serious."

"Yes." She looked from face to face. "Why is that funny?"

"Well, it's just…" One of the women looked between them. "I mean, you work? *Why?*" She seemed genuinely perplexed. "You're married."

Leon drew a tested breath.

"She just had a daughter," his mother reminded. "Tanja isn't working right now."

"Oh, of course. Well done on getting your figure back."

His mother smoothly shifted them along to the next group, saving Leon from having to blister the ears of a stranger. He loosely encircled Tanja's wrist and felt the way her pulse was racing. Her gaze was darting like a mouse seeking a safe path through a roomful of cats. He wove their fingers together and tried to convey that he would keep her safe.

She brightened slightly as she was asked where she was from.

"Tofino," she replied with obvious fondness. "It's a small fishing and whale-watching town on the West Coast of Canada."

"Oh, yes. We stopped there once when we were sailing. A bohemian little place," one woman told the rest of the group. "Pretty enough to visit, but I can't imagine growing up there." She gave a small shudder.

"Greta," Leon warned the woman against being so rude.

"Many of my friends couldn't wait to get away," Tanja said with forced lightness. "It's a place you don't appreciate until you no longer have it. Will you excuse me a moment?" She extricated her fingers from his. "I want to call the nanny. Make sure everything is going well."

Tanja was so far out of her depth she was hyperventilating. Drowning.

Leaving.

"Tanja." Leon was right behind her as she reached the threshold.

"I can't do this," she said in subdued panic.

"It shouldn't have been this." He shot an impatient look back to the party. "But it's only a few hours."

"This." She waved between them. "I can't believe I thought I could even *pretend* to be your wife—"

He caught her hand as comprehension flared in his eyes. His mouth firmed and he pushed her into a powder room, closing the door on them.

Tanja had a brief impression of ivory wallpaper with silver stripes and roses, gold fixtures and burning candles that gave off a scent of bergamot and lavender, then Leon was all that was in her senses. Tall and intimidating, broad and commanding.

"What happened? What did she say?" His tone nearly took out her knees.

"Nothing! It's all of this." She waved a hand toward the rooms they'd left and the one they were in.

"I mean, I knew I wasn't in your league when we first got together. That's why I expected it to be an affair. And I get it now, why you left me, but I thought I could at least pretend we're happily married for Il-li's sake. I just feel like such an *idiot*, though. Such a milkmaid to your—"

"Stop it." He caught her elbow, stilling her flailing gestures, not hurting but firm. Forcing her to look at him and pay attention.

He was the one who wasn't paying attention!

"I don't fit *in*, Leon." She tried to shake off his grip as though she could shake reality into him. "I'll do anything for Illi, but I can't act like I belong here." Hot tears of despair hit the backs of her eyes. "No one is going to believe you want *me*."

"I do want you. Exactly as you are." A fierce light flared to life behind his gaze as he drew her into him with a small crash of their bodies. *"You know that."*

"How?"

"It doesn't matter how. It just is. Feel it." His mouth burned across hers in one hot sweep, then another. "It's here. It's always been here," he muttered between kisses that tasted of anger, but not a kind that was directed at her. His hands were gentle but hard. Imperative. "It has to be you."

Her heart fell, and she tried to find emotional purchase on unsteady ground, but there was none. All of her felt unbalanced.

Helplessly, she clung to him. Slipped her arms beneath the open edges of his suit jacket, curling them around his waist while he pulled her in for a deeper, longer, harder kiss. One that took and gave and was so rife with layers of emotion, it softened her knees.

Amid the taste of anguish and desperation, yearning and his irrepressible will, physical craving crept in, making each kiss last longer. Flow deeper. Their hands roamed in anxious apology and hunger to connect, rebuilding the tenuous threads that bound them.

She slid her hand down to cup him through his trousers. He was hard and hissed under her exploring touch.

"Do you want me to…?" She glanced toward the door as her fingers sought the tab on his fly.

"I want *you*," he growled, reaching back to click the lock. "Isn't that obvious?" He reached into an inner pocket of his jacket and set a condom next to the sink.

She widened her eyes, unable to hold back a choking laugh. "You brought that to dinner with your *mother*?"

"If I learned nothing else in our marriage, it was to always carry one when I'm with you because we can't keep our hands off one another." He crowded her toward the sink.

Her heart was still fluttering, bubbles of laughter rising in her along with a deep craving for reassurance. She needed this. Needed to feel irresistible. Needed the reflection of hunger in him that matched her own urgent desire to break down their barriers and be completely intimate.

The vanity was too small to sit on. He turned her

to face it. Her eyes widened in the mirror as he guided her hands to splay flat upon it. Then he ran his hands down her sides, shaping her hips and coming back up to fondle her breasts.

"Sometimes I think you have a very dirty mind," she accused on a pleasured gasp, arching into his palms, pushing her backside into the hardness behind his fly. "That all you think about is sex and what we'll do next."

"Only sometimes?" His hands were slipping into her cleavage, warming and awakening her, making her breaths catch. "It's not sex I think about. It's *you*."

She shivered, possibly from his words, possibly from the way he teased her nipples before moving down her sides again, adjusting her, using his feet to nudge hers apart while his gaze stayed glued to hers, making sure she was with him for every breath and caress.

She was. It was blatant and lewd and they should have gone upstairs to the privacy of his penthouse, but the immediacy of their desire heartened her. It was as comforting as it was exciting. Part of her knew that it wasn't a strength to be this physically weak, but she drank in the fact he was as anxious to be joined with her as she was. It erased the deep sense of inequality that had been hitting her again and again all day.

His hands went farther down her hips to her thighs. Her dress came up with the next caress of his hands upward, smoothing over her thighs and hips and up to her waist.

"No, keep looking at me," he said in a jagged

voice, forcing her to blink her heavy eyelids back open. "I like watching you lose focus."

She licked her lips, watching the heat gathering in his gaze as his caresses grew more flagrant, slipping down the front of her lace underwear and—

"Oh!"

"Eyes open, lovely," he commanded in a hypnotic tone. His free hand stole around to fondle her breast again. "Good?"

"You know it is," she panted. His touch was moving easily in the slick moisture he'd called forth.

"The only person you have to fit with is me. Understand? And we fit perfectly, Tanja. We always have. Yes?"

"Yes," she moaned, unable to resist rocking her hips to seek a firmer touch. Her eyelashes were fluttering as exquisite ripples of arousal rolled upward from his touch.

"Not pretending now, are you?"

"No," she said on a shaken laugh.

He released her, staying close enough behind her she felt the brush of his hand against her cheeks, the rough-soft wool of his trousers as he opened them. The hot weight of his naked erection rested against her cheek while he opened the condom. He applied it and she watched his gaze stay down, admiring her buttocks as he palmed her curves.

"This is terrible," she said, coming back to awareness of where they were. "We shouldn't be doing this here."

"Do you want to wait?" His eyes met hers and his

wicked fingertip swept beneath her thong, teasing the swollen bundle of nerves at the top of her sex.

She shuddered in pleasure, her voice catching as she admitted, "No." She couldn't wait another second.

"Good." He moved the placket aside. "Eyes open," he reminded her huskily, then guided himself, seeking and pressing.

"Leon," she sighed as he began to breach her. He rocked lightly in small thrusts that took him a little deeper with each one.

"Battle conditions, lovely," he said as he coaxed inexorably for her to take all of him. "Fast and quiet." He held her gaze as he leaned forward to press his open mouth against her nape. His hand slipped in the front of her underwear again. "Can you do that?"

"No. Yes. Leon," she moaned softly.

He played with her, making pleasure spike upward. Making her dance her hips back into his, urging him to move.

He did, and the friction was as inciting as it was rough.

She wanted to close her eyes so bad. This was too intimate, but she needed the visual connection as much as the physical. Needed to see him come undone even as her own vision blurred, eyes dampening as her arousal increased.

She bit back her most lurid noises, but couldn't help pushing her hips back into his, wanting the subdued slam that seemed to reverberate joyous sensations through her whole body. When they were like this, nothing else mattered. They were perfectly, utterly aligned.

"Tell me when," he said in a jagged voice.

"Now. I'm ready. I'm... *Now*," she gasped as her climax rose up to engulf her.

The heel of his palm stayed firm against her mound as his other hand took hold of her shoulder. He thrust hard and fast a few more times before he held himself deep inside her while his whole body shuddered.

He pulsed and throbbed within her, teeth clenched. His cheeks flushed dark, and his glittering gaze kept possession of her own.

CHAPTER EIGHT

"Don't we have to go back?" Tanja asked when Leon drew her from the powder room and out his mother's doors toward the elevator.

"No." Leon knew he sounded like a Neanderthal, but his heart was still unsteady and, despite his powerful orgasm, his throat tight. He couldn't stop hearing Tanja's distressed *I can't do this.*

She had hurried to tidy her makeup, but she was pale beneath her flush of culmination. Her gaze on him as they entered the elevator was apprehensive.

He reassured her the only way he knew how, by dragging her close and kissing her until she melted. When he lifted his head, the wariness in her eyes was replaced with golden lights of yearning, the ones that urged him closer. Invited him to touch and hold her.

That's what he needed to ease this monster inside him. That quiet surrender of herself to him.

When they entered his penthouse, Valerie poked her head from the kitchen in surprise.

"Call my mother. Let her know Tanja is unwell," he said.

"Of course. May I get you anything?"

"I'm fine," Tanja murmured, sending him a doleful look for his lie.

"You've been unwell," he justified as he steered her down the hall. "And you weren't enjoying it."

"What exactly are you referring to?"

His mouth twitched and his tension eased. If she was making jokes, they were okay.

He had heard himself in her compulsion to flee, though. He had done the same thing for years, absenting himself from Greece however he had to. It had hit him hard that she wanted to flee *him* in that same way—as if he was causing her the emotional angst he had endured through his childhood.

They checked on a sleeping Illi and Tanja told the nanny she could leave for the evening. She brought the baby monitor into the master bedroom with them.

"I feel bad for ducking out on your mother," she said as they undressed. "Cowardly."

"Don't."

"Leon—"

"No, listen." He yanked his shirt from his trousers. "You should have had this life all along." He waved at the professionally decorated room with its satin drapes and silk area rug and bamboo sheets. "Get used to it because this is your life now, even after our divorce."

"But I don't *want*—"

"Tanja! *I* was pretending when we married. I pretended it didn't matter that I wasn't taking it seriously.

That it was okay to leave you with nothing. Let me fix that much."

She was in bare feet, hair loose, hugging a silk kimono closed across her nudity.

"Maybe I even pretended…" He paced away, embarrassed to admit he'd wanted to be like her. Warm and sincere and surrounded by open affection. "It was never about *you* not being good enough for *me*."

There was a long, pensive silence before she said quietly, "I still can't help feeling I'm not—"

He pivoted to face her and cut her off. "You went to a foreign country to teach women how to be as financially independent as you are. You fostered a baby and now you're a mother. What makes you think you can't walk into a cocktail party of blowhards and hold your own? Win them over?"

"Fear," she admitted glumly.

"Well, stop it," he chided. "You're actually very brave and bright and likable. If anyone insults your hometown or tries to make you feel small again, say something about the yacht. That usually snaps people into their best behavior, in hopes of earning an invitation."

She snorted. "You do have a mean streak, don't you?"

"I come by it honestly." It should have been a lighthearted rejoinder, but it was too true. His father had held out carrots like that, playing with people's hopes, manipulating them with the promise of rewards that hadn't arrived.

When he looked at her again, her teasing smile had faded into a troubled frown.

"My biggest problem is figuring out what's real and what's pretend. Sometimes this feels very..."

He nodded, accepting that even as it caused a jolt of guilty conscience.

"I led you on the first time. I wish you could understand how angry I am with myself for that." The words came from the depth of his chest, scoring behind his breastbone like sandpaper and leaving a scrape in the back of his throat. "That's why I'm trying to be as truthful as possible now. I don't want to hurt you again."

"I know." She nodded jerkily, her lips clamped to withstand some inner agony. "But you will anyway."

That broadsword went through him so cleanly he could only hiss as it eviscerated him.

"I'm going to take off my makeup." She moved into the bathroom while he stood there frozen in torment. Absorbing the knowledge that she could—and would—hurt him, too.

"I've asked Demitri to reschedule all of your appointments today," Leon said over breakfast the next morning. "I heard what you said last night. This is a lot to adjust to. I'll go into the office and the staff will be out. Take the day to get your bearings."

Great. All the time in the world to dwell and brood and fret over the way they'd come together in a clash. She could pick apart the contradiction of a man who was capable of showing incredible care and concern, who delivered indescribable pleasure, offered remorse over the way they'd parted and said he wanted to make things up to her, but withheld himself.

Refused to open his heart.

She'd been up in the early hours to settle Illi. When she'd come back to bed, he'd spooned her into him, but that cuddle had turned into lazy, wordless lovemaking. He'd risen a few hours later when Illi stirred, leaving Tanja fast asleep and unaware he was even gone.

He could be so considerate and tender. It was no wonder she was beginning to tip into falling for him again, but even his offer to leave her at home alone felt like a withdrawal of sorts. A distance he was putting between them on purpose.

"No?" he prompted at her silence.

"No. I mean yes. Thank you." She smiled as a thought surfaced. "I could call Shonda."

"That reminds me." He rose and came back with a stack of electronic devices. They were programmed with emails and numbers to reach him, his PA, and all his key staff.

She might have refused, but having a laptop would allow her to put out feelers for work. It felt a little defeatist to cold-bloodedly plan her life after her divorce, when they could be married for a year or more, but she accepted everything gracefully.

Once everyone was gone, she spoke to her family, then sent an email to Kahina that included a selfie with Illi. She asked after Kahina's family and let her friend know she and Illi were well and that Georgiou might be in touch as he worked on the legalities of

Illi's adoption. Tanja also left messages on Brahim's stale social media accounts, urging him to get in touch when he could.

After that, she wallowed in the quiet of the penthouse, enjoying coffee outside before she sorted through some of the outfits in the spare bedroom and moved a few casual pieces into the section of the master bedroom closet that Leon had set aside for her. She had just fed Illi and was considering her options for lunch, Illi on her hip, when the landline rang.

"Hello?" she asked cautiously, belatedly realizing she should have said it in Greek.

"Tanja, it's Ophelia. I wondered if I might come up and meet the baby?"

"Um." *Don't be a coward.* "Of course. Um. We would love that. When were you thinking?"

"Would now be convenient?"

Tanja looked from Illi's soggy chin to her own comfortable but threadbare shorts and T-shirt. "Of course," she said with false brightness.

She had just enough time to wash her daughter's face and slip into a simple yet pretty summer dress, then pull her hair into a ponytail before there was a brief knock.

Tanja set Illi under her play set and hurried to let Ophelia in.

Ophelia looked as intimidatingly put together as she had last night, this time in a linen pantsuit with an emerald green blouse. Her hair was pinned in a smooth chignon, her makeup flawless.

"The housekeeper is out, I'm afraid, but I could

make coffee and find some cookies?" Tanja offered as she led Ophelia into the lounge. "I should have called you myself this morning, to apologize for not staying last night. I, um, wasn't feeling well."

Ophelia gave her a steady look that was even more piercing and unreadable than her son's. "Leon has already explained that you weren't feeling welcome."

"That's not...quite true." Tanja flexed her linked fingers. "Out of my depth is a better way of putting it. This is all very overwhelming."

Ophelia halted to stare at Illi on the blanket on the floor.

"This is Illi." What had Leon told his mother about her parentage?

"She could be Leon's, couldn't she? With that coloring?" Ophelia's expression softened almost imperceptibly as she shifted to perch on the edge of a cushion, her attention remaining on the baby, while Illi batted at the toys dangling from the play set propped over her.

Tanja sank into the chair opposite, surprised and not sure how much she should reveal.

"Please don't be alarmed. Leon wouldn't have told me if he didn't trust me to keep the information to myself. We have our difficulties and I was shocked to learn he'd been married all this time, but he wouldn't lie to me about having a child."

"I very much appreciate the lengths he's been willing to go to help me keep her," Tanja said tentatively.

Ophelia studied her for a long moment, looking as

though she wanted to say something. A small frown dented her expression.

"I disappointed him by inviting a crowd last night," she finally decided to say. "We have a relationship that is… I find it easier to have people around. A buffer." Her brief smile was deeply pained, then gone. "It's an old habit, but it wasn't fair to you. I apologize."

"That's not necessary, but thank you." Tanja's heart instinctively went out to her, reaching across the space that felt like a chasm because Ophelia was clearly clinging hard to her side, terrified to reach out.

Illi was kicking and grabbing at the toys, burbling away, easier to watch than looking at each other, so they did that for a few minutes.

Tanja snuck glances at Ophelia, though, and watched as her expression grew poignant. Her hand twitched and she leaned forward a little, almost as if she wanted to bend and reach out, catch at a flailing foot, but she seemed to think better of it and straightened again.

I think she quit showing affection for me so he wouldn't use me against her.

Tanja's heart clutched. "Would you like to hold her?"

"Best not to get attached," Ophelia said with a valiant smile. "Leon tells me this isn't a permanent arrangement." She met Tanja's gaze, and that suggestion of words wanting to be spoken was there again. This time she was a little braver, her voice holding a hint of emotion. "I take heart from the fact he's come this far. Until his call the other day, I was convinced he would never marry or have children. Even... Well, baby steps as they say."

"Wait until you see him with her," Tanja said with emotion-laden humor. "He's so sweet, you'll die."

"Oh, he won't let me see that," Ophelia assured her with another of those smiles that painted over what Tanja was beginning to realize was profound pain. "He was torn last night, afraid to hover over you too closely in case I guessed how much you mean to him. The lecture this morning was very telling, though." Her mouth twitched.

"What did he say?" Tanja asked with a rise and fall of hope and dread. "Whatever it was, I'm sorry. Honestly, I was overreacting. Suffering a case of imposter syndrome."

"Nonsense." Ophelia held up a hand. "You are not an imposter, and his anger isn't anything I don't deserve. I'm extremely sensitive to any sort of disapproval or criticism from him, though." She tucked her hands in her lap. "My first instinct is to protect myself proactively, thus the crowd. It always goes wrong, of course, but he does the same with me. The fact he kept his marriage from me for five years tells me how much you meant to him."

So many words of protest and correction jammed into Tanja's throat that she couldn't make any of them come out in a sensible way. They simply sat there with their sharp edges, suffocating her while Ophelia flicked a speck of lint from her sleeve.

"I had hoped after his father passed that Leon and I would develop a new understanding between us, but—" Her sigh was the epitome of despair. "Leon was faced with incredibly difficult challenges. I didn't help. I pushed him so hard to fight for what was rightfully his. If I'd known he had a wife to go back to… Well, I don't know what I would have done," she admitted heavily. "I can see now he was angry over what he was forced to give up in order to stay here. I won't say he blamed me," Ophelia continued in a tone of reflection. "But he must have seen me as part of the reason he was forced to stay here instead of returning to you. That's why we haven't been able to mend things."

"I'm so s—"

"Please." Ophelia forestalled her with a smooth show of her palm. "You are not the source of my troubles with my son. That lies entirely with me."

"I think you're being very hard on yourself," Tanja said tentatively. "Leon has only said a few things about his early years, but I get the sense there was quite a bit of tension. That your husband was a difficult person and bears much of the responsibility."

"You're very generous. I can see why Leon is so attracted to you. His father was a terrible bully, but I can't say I was at my best in the way I chose to fight him. I sank to his level far too often. When it comes to Leon, I'm reaping what was sown."

"Well, you can sow new things," Tanja said earnestly. "I hope you see me and Illi as a fresh field. You and I don't have to let any of those old weeds grow between us. We can define our relationship however it suits us."

Ophelia didn't say anything for a long minute, but

a faint sheen of tears seemed to glimmer in her eyes. Her mouth might have trembled. It was hard to tell. She was very good at hiding her emotions.

"It would mean a lot to me if you and I were to become friends. It's difficult to feel close to my son."

You love him, Tanja wanted to say, but she had the feeling it was the sort of incantation that wasn't allowed to be spoken aloud in Leon's world for fear of breaking a spell. It explained so much about him.

"We are friends," Tanja assured her huskily. "Please join us anytime."

Leon was both pleased and disgruntled at his mother visiting, proclaiming, "She owed you an apology, but she had no right to invite herself into our home." Then he added gruffly, "How was it?"

"It was nice," Tanja said, privately breathless over him saying "our" home.

Everything seemed to be smoothed over two nights later when they invited Ophelia and Cornelius to dine with them. Cornelius was comfortable to be around, engaging and easygoing and smitten with Ophelia. She wasn't the most effusive person. Her tension around Leon seemed to feed his own so there was a constant static in the air, but she seemed sincere in her desire for Tanja to feel more comfortable in her world and offered gentle advice.

Ophelia's support bolstered Tanja's confidence when she and Leon attended Georgiou's wife's fundraiser.

Tanja kept hoping she and Leon would find a comfortable set of boundaries, clear lines they couldn't cross, but they were blurry and forever shifting. They made love before they dressed and sent each other sly looks filled with sizzling memory, but she had to keep reminding herself this wasn't real. Tanja could put on a figure-hugging strapless gown in diaphanous pink with gorgeous beadwork in metallic silver and rose gold, but that didn't make her Leon's wife any more than it made her the movie star who ought to be wearing this for her own performance.

No one else seemed to notice she was a phony, though. She received dozens of compliments and was warmly welcomed by everyone they met.

It helped that Leon never left her side, ensuring any awkward questions were quickly fielded and the conversation steered into neutral topics. Overall, it was a pleasant evening, and she was even invited to join the board of directors for the foundation that Georgiou's wife ran.

"Do you want to do that sort of work?" Leon asked when she mentioned it the next day. "Because I have two corporate boards I could put you on immediately if you're interested. Paid, not volunteer."

"I don't want you to give me some placeholder job out of nepotism."

"Tanja." He clicked off his tablet. "You have a degree in accounting. You're not only qualified to provide knowledge and oversight, I *trust* you. One of the organizations I'm thinking of is run by a CEO who worked for my father. He wouldn't be with us if I had reason to distrust him, but extra reassurances are always appreciated. The other has a young woman at the helm who has star power, but she could use support while she finds her feet. Having another woman with solid business sense as a sounding board would set her up for success."

"You really trust me that much?" She was ridiculously flattered.

"Are there stages of trust? I thought it was one or the other and, yes, I trust you." He seemed to brace himself. "Don't you trust me?"

"Of course. I—" The words *I love you* caught in her throat, causing a full-body sting at holding back the enormous surge of emotion. Maybe she didn't entirely trust him. There *were* levels of trust. She knew she was physically safe with him. She would entrust her daughter's life, as well as her own, to him, but she wasn't sure how he would react if she made her declaration aloud.

Actually, maybe she knew him well enough—trusted him enough—to be confident he would withdraw from such a declaration and look pained at not being able to reciprocate.

"You what?" he prompted, touching her cheek to coax her face up so she couldn't avoid his searching gaze.

Her heart was right there, pounding in her throat.

"I do trust you. And the job sounds interesting, but what happens when…" She swallowed, voice fading to a husk. "When we're over?"

A flicker of something bleak flashed in his eyes

before he dropped his hand and hooded his thoughts behind an impassive expression.

"That could be a year or two from now. You shouldn't put your career on hold if you want to pursue it. This would be valuable experience. If the postings interest you, take them."

He sent her the details a little while later. One was a solar power corporation, the other a fair trade importer. Both were different enough from anything she'd taken on before to be intriguing and challenging. Commitment-wise, the demands would be light enough to fit around Illi's needs and dovetail with her social obligations with Leon.

Things fell into place very quickly. Soon Tanja was dressing in a business suit once or twice a week to attend meetings. She spent another in jeans and a T-shirt, answering emails and reviewing reports, then put on couture for evenings with Leon. When he had commitments in Rome, they took *Poseidon's Crown* since Illi's passport situation hadn't been sorted yet and anchored offshore.

When Leon had meetings in Singapore, he went alone. Tanja had feared she would feel like a guest if he wasn't here with them, but the penthouse was beginning to feel like her home. Like *their* home. Illi's room was a proper nursery with duckling wallpaper and an infant swing, a play saucer and every other toy Leon could find online. Tanja had a desk of her own in Leon's office, and they often worked there very companionably.

She missed him intensely while he was gone,

though, and had to fight saying so when he called her over the tablet. She missed him because she loved him. She couldn't deny it when it overwhelmed her in waves of euphoric angst. When her daughter tried to drop her face through the tablet screen to get to him and Tanja wanted to do the very same thing.

Perhaps he missed them, too. He walked in late on a Wednesday evening when she hadn't been expecting him until Thursday afternoon. He surprised her in her pj's watching an old rom-com, fighting her lonesomeness with a glass of wine and a bowl of popcorn.

He exhaled a huge sigh as he saw her. Before she could do more than set aside the bowl and rise to say, "You're home," he had planted a kiss on her that nearly made her faint.

Heart hammering, exchanging no other words, they peeked in on the sleeping Illi, then hurried to the master bedroom where they ravaged the hell out of each other. When he reached for the nightstand, she said, "It's okay. I saw the doctor. I have an IUD."

He fell on her and their naked joining took them to a new level of intimate pleasure, one that left her in a state of elation for days after.

Tanja began to believe he was coming to love her, too. Maybe, despite all the trials and tribulations and the five years of separation, she was married to her soul mate?

Leon sorted through the courier envelopes on his desk, separating out the ones addressed to him from the ones addressed to his wife.

He had half expected to feel bothered by sharing his home. He'd never lived with anyone so closely and had always liked his space just so.

Tanja was fairly tidy by nature, but her cosmetics turned up on his side of the bathroom sink and her purse landed on his desk and sometimes the shirt he wanted was already on her back. As for Illi, she had a very attentive nanny, but still needed a lot of care and attention, often at the most inconvenient times, and for someone who had only mastered rolling, she was very good at scattering toys far and wide.

He had missed that small sense of disarray while he'd been away on his business trip. He should have embraced the time alone. He'd always preferred to answer to no one, but he'd been irritated that Tanja and Illi hadn't been able to come with him. He had felt as though he was holding his breath the whole time, annoyed at the way people rushed to do his bidding while each minute of the clock dragged.

The last thing he wanted was to become dependent, but he had rushed back early. Which disconcerted him. Tanja was the furthest thing from cruel, but she didn't have to be. She had the power to hurt him anyway, and that knowledge, that anticipation that she would, hung over him like a blade that could drop at any second.

It whistled down upon him when he opened the envelope from Georgiou.

"How would you feel if I invited my father to visit?" Tanja asked, coming in while he was still absorbing what his lawyer had sent.

Leon's blood was pounding so hard in his ears he barely heard her.

"What's wrong?" Her tone plummeted into something cold and filled with dread.

He gave himself a mental shake, wiping his face clean of whatever was causing her cheeks to grow hollow and her eyes to widen with apprehension.

"Nothing," he stated. It felt like a lie. A grave one. "Georgiou's email the other day said things were going well with the officials in Istuval. He said we should have something soon. I thought this was the finalized postnuptial, but it's also Illi's adoption papers." He showed her the official certificates.

Tanja's eyes latched on to the Canadian passport and she snatched it up. "Oh, my God! When he asked me to get her photo taken for this, I thought it would take weeks."

She flipped it open, saw Illi's name and clasped the passport to her heart. Her eyes welled. "She's mine? Really? Oh, my God, Leon. Thank you. *Thank you.*"

She hurried around to throw herself against him in a shaking mass of every emotion—joy and relief and things he couldn't identify.

"It's okay." Leon reflexively closed his arms around her and ran soothing hands over her back. "Yes, she's yours now."

"I feel terrible for being this happy," she said through her sniffles. "I mean, her mother should have her, right? And Brahim is still out there—"

"You're still allowed to be happy, Tanja." He wondered sometimes how such a slender body could contain such a big heart. "You want her to be safe and loved, and she is."

"I just wish I could give him this, too. Bring him with us when we take Illi h-home."

He stiffened slightly.

She felt it and jerked her head up, fighting to get hold of her emotions. "We *are* taking her home, aren't we?"

He was tempted, so tempted to give in to what he wanted despite knowing it was the worst possible thing he could do to her. He refused to lead her on again, though. No matter how much he wanted to let this play out until what could only be a bitter end.

"*You* are." His body was bracing so hard against the inevitable pain that was coming that he felt as though hairline fractures were creeping through his limbs and torso and neck.

"But—" Here came the hurt, the flash of betrayal that cut him in half, the profound anguish that filled him with guilt. "What do you mean? We're a family. Aren't we?"

His arms wanted to squeeze her in, but he made himself drop them away.

"You and Illi are. It's time you took her to meet the rest of yours."

"But—"

"This is what we knew would happen, Tanja." He spoke over her. "It happened sooner than later. That's good. I'm glad you didn't have to wait years to know she's indisputably your daughter. But this is what we agreed, that you would take her home when the time came."

"But I don't *have to*, Leon! I mean, I want to go home. I miss everyone and I want to meet my nephew and introduce Illi to everyone, but we could *all* go. And then—"

She stopped speaking, not saying aloud that they could come back here.

Because he was already dismissing the notion with a pained shake of his head.

"Think about this clearly, Tanja. This is the best outcome. It's not a fight. We're ending things on a civil note with a clean settlement already worked out." He waved at his desk where the postnuptial contract sat, thick and heavy and not nearly as satisfying as he had anticipated.

"So I'm supposed to just *leave*? With Illi? And we'll never talk to one another again? You don't even care that I'm taking her away from you?"

That was a knife to the vitals that gave such a hard wrench he could hardly breathe. He waved again at the document he had thought would make all of this easy, but it wasn't easy at all. He had to fight to hold on to a level tone.

"I have the right to expect regular updates. Photos and occasional visits." It wasn't enough. He already felt cheated. "We'll each provide for her in our own way, but we're both ensuring she has the best life we're capable of offering."

"And that's enough for you?" she cried with disbelief, backing off a few steps as though she could hardly take in all the ways he was disappointing her. "A couple of photos and the assurance that she'll have a good education is all you want from either of us? Don't you feel anything else? You acted like I was your salvation the other night!"

It had felt that way, and that was why he had to let her go before he couldn't.

"The goal was to end this on a civilized note," he reminded her, dredging up the cool ruthlessness he'd been raised on. "Can we?"

She flinched at his tone, making him feel like a bastard, but that was exactly why they had to end this. How did she not see that, eventually, this was what their marriage would devolve into, only so much worse?

Tanja stood before him with her hands in knotted fists, her body trembling with impotence, mouth working with hurt. Angry tears in her eyes.

"You have put me in an impossible position, Leon." Her voice was thick with outrage. "If I fight for you, for *us*, you'll see it as me trying to prolong this argument, which will only drive you away. So fine. I won't fight. If you want me to leave, I will. As soon as I can book a flight. But know this." She held up a trembling finger. "I am leaving *because*… I love you. I'm doing this *for* you, because I want to give you the thing you think will make you happy."

She started to walk out, paused at the door.

"But I won't wait five years again."

Leon spent the next weeks traveling. Each time he walked into his empty penthouse, he couldn't stand the silence, the lack of clutter or the profound absence.

He found excuse after excuse to leave town, but only felt emptier and emptier as time wore on.

Tanja, damn her, had sent one text to say they'd landed safely and nothing else.

He hadn't reached out, either. They were back to the stalemate of their first five years of marriage.

Until she ended that, too.

When Georgiou sent him the notice that she'd finalized the papers and taken Leon's ten-million-euro settlement, Leon was knocked onto his ass. He sat down to get drunk and couldn't even do that. He just sat there with his bottle of ouzo on the coffee table, staring at the spot on the carpet where Illi had spit up and left a stain.

He should only feel satisfaction that she had taken the money. He wanted to provide for her and Illi, and some integral part of him was pleased he was able to do that much for them, but he genuinely hadn't expected her to take his money.

Even though she had told him she wouldn't wait for him, he hadn't expected her to end it. That was the stark truth. She had said she loved him, and some distant part of him had known in those seconds that he loved her, too. That the emotional connection between them would never die. It couldn't.

He had also known he didn't deserve her. *He* was the one who'd been in the impossible position. If he gave in to longing and let their marriage go on, he would only be proving what a selfish self-serving ass he really was—exactly like his father.

Letting her go had been the only way to prove he was worthy of the love she'd offered him.

But she had gone through with the divorce. Why? To be free of him, as she'd once told him she wanted to be? Had her love died that quickly?

Unable to bear his own brooding, he abruptly had the helicopter take him to the island where he'd spent his earliest years. This was his mother's domain, where his father had mostly left her alone.

Leon's first thought on landing was to wonder what Tanja would think of it. Why hadn't he brought her here? It was pretty and quiet and might have quelled some of her homesickness, given its seaside location. The beach was beautiful. Once Illi was walking, they could have enjoyed it to no end.

If they'd been a family.

They weren't in his life anymore. It was such a punch in the chest each time he faced it that he could hardly stay on his feet. Illi wouldn't smile at him like he was a white night rescuing her from a tower when he walked in to collect her from her crib. Tanja wouldn't set him aflame with a sexy glance or make him laugh out of the blue or settle against him on the sofa and just make everything in his world…right.

"Leon." His mother gave him a frown that might have indicated concern if they were the type to express that sort of thing toward one another. "How was London?"

"Hmm? Oh. I don't know." He supposed that's where he'd been. It was all such a blur. "Cornelius here?" he asked politely.

"He's staking the tomatoes. You walked right by him, said hello and asked what kind they were. What's wrong?" Her dark brows drew together.

"Nothing," he insisted, trying to convince himself it was true. "Tanja and I are officially divorced. I thought I should tell you."

"I know. I'm so sorry."

That took him aback. "How do you know?" Was it on the gossip sites *already*? How humiliating.

"We video chat." His mother clasped her hands and pressed her lips into a self-conscious line. "Tanja said she wasn't certain you would tell me and thought I should know."

Leon swore and flung himself to face the window, then veered out the doors to the terrace, uncomfortable with his mother seeing how tortured he was by all of this. He braced his fists on the stone balustrade and stared at the green-blue sea, but he couldn't have picked out if there were boats upon it or giant squids. His entire body was aching. Writhing in agony.

"Are you angry I've kept contact with her?" his mother asked warily as she came to stand beside him. "It seemed rude to ignore her."

He choked at that, thinking his ignoring Tanja for five years was a lot worse than rude. It had been self-destructive madness.

Something in her hesitant tone plucked at an old, tight line of hurt inside him. She had never been able to make a right step around his father and neither had he. It was a reminder of exactly what he was trying to avoid.

"It's fine, Mother." He had to fight to keep the anger with himself out of his voice so she wouldn't think it was directed at her. "I'm glad that you're staying in touch. How is she?" His ears were reaching for her words before she spoke.

"They seem well, but Tanja doesn't seem very happy."

I'm doing this for you.

Then why did it feel like she was doing it *to* him?

He hung his head. Some twisted voice inside him was convinced she was hurting him on purpose because that's what married people did to one another, didn't they? Tanja wouldn't, though. He knew that. In his heart of hearts, he knew she wasn't like that.

"I'm glad you're not angry." His mother's voice wasn't quite steady. "Because..." She sounded so fearful. "Well, I quite like her, Leon. It's nice to see the baby, too. I'm genuinely sorry things didn't work out." After another pause, she said quietly, "I blame myself."

"Don't." He didn't even know what he was trying to forestall with that blunt word. An apology? Being forced to acknowledge his own culpability in how they'd let his father damage them? He didn't want to examine their baggage. He never, ever wanted to have uncomfortable conversations about feelings, especially with her. There were too many. It would take too long and hurt too much.

"I thought I was standing up for myself with your father," she said, voice almost a plea.

She lightly touched his arm, but he didn't look

at her. Couldn't. His heart was being crushed and squeezed and liable to burst under the pressure.

"I was young and felt responsible for keeping all of this for *you*. I didn't care that *I* was unhappy, but I see now that I caused you to think we're not the type of people who are allowed to be happy. That we're not lovable. We are, Leon." Her touch squeezed his forearm. "It's taken a lot of convincing, but Cornelius has made me believe that I'm worthy of being loved, and so are you."

"*You* are," he agreed stiffly. "But I was careless with her. I was filled with a sense of entitlement and threw her away like she didn't matter. I'm no better than he was—"

"You are a million times better than he was," his mother broke in vehemently. "I stand in awe of the man you've become *in spite* of the example that was set for you. My greatest regret is that I let him come between you and I, leaving you thinking a woman's love isn't steadfast. It is, Leon. I have always loved you. And so does Tanja."

But she divorced me.

I'm doing this for you.

His heart lurched. He couldn't bear this. Could she be right, though? Was there hope?

His mother's hand was clutched so tightly to his arm he was compelled to set his arm around her and draw her into his side. He held her as she began to weep into his shoulder.

"It's okay," he murmured, exactly as he would comfort Illi or Tanja or anyone else he loved. After a moment, he set his cheek on her hair. His misted gaze fell on the heavyset man propping up tomatoes in the garden.

Cornelius nodded approval.

Believing his ex-wife might still love him was one thing. Going to Canada to talk her into coming back into his life was quite another. Tanja was completely within her right to invite him to go to hell. He had pushed her out of his life twice. Why would she trust him a third time?

Nevertheless, Leon flew into Vancouver and chartered a seaplane from there. It landed at the marina he would have partially owned had his father not died when he had.

As he stepped onto the wharf and saw the fresh signage going up that read Melha Marina he stood there for a full minute, hands on his hips. The widest, most foolish grin split his face and refused to stop.

That's why she'd taken the settlement. Of course, she hadn't kept it. He couldn't be happier that she had divorced him if that was why she'd done it.

He walked up to a building that was in the process of being returned to its original blue and white. Inside, a man about his age stood with a baby strapped to his chest like the kid was a smoke jumper and Zach the parachute.

Zach pointed out something on a drawing and gave a woman in a yellow hardhat instructions on finding the property line. When he rolled the drawing and handed it to the woman, they both turned to the open door where Leon stood.

His old friend's surprised expression slammed shut. "Leon. What brings you here?"

Leon stepped aside to let the woman leave. "I'm looking for Tanja." Obviously.

Zach stiffened. "Is the money not coming through again?"

"It's *through*. Hers. Yours, I guess." Leon glanced around the interior of the office where he had first met "Books." Tanja had said something snappy to her brother, turning from a cabinet and going very coltish and still. The zing of attraction as she met Leon's eyes had been so undeniable and visceral, he was still trying to breathe through the power of it today.

"It's hers," Zach said. "She wanted it for Dad. I agreed to run it."

Leon dragged his attention back to Zach's hostile glare. "Look. I know I owe you an apology. I sincerely regret that our deal fell apart. I don't know if Tanja has explained—"

"What's to explain?" Zach shrugged it off. "You warned me to wait until the money was yours, but I didn't. Dad told me I was moving too fast. Even Books had concerns about how much debt I was racking up. I didn't listen. I crashed and burned and it sucked, but live and learn, right?" He didn't sound particularly bitter, just fatalistic.

"If that's how you feel…" Leon grabbed the edge of the door. "Why do you hate my guts?"

"Because you broke my little sister's heart, jackass. *Twice*."

* * *

Tanja was half-heartedly reviewing three different job offers when there was a knock on her door at the bottom of the stairs.

She presumed it was Shonda, but her sister-in-law usually let herself in, calling hello as she came up. They were becoming like true sisters, confiding their new mother failures and triumphs, cuddling each other's infants as often as their own.

Tanja veered minute by minute between so much happiness she could hardly contain it, and such a profound sadness it was all she could do to breathe. She was exhausted and heartbroken and determined to pick up the pieces and move on anyway.

Shonda didn't appear, and another knock sounded.

Tanja rose and slipped down the stairs, glancing into Illi's crib on her way. She was fast asleep, taking to her new home the way she'd taken to all the other changes she'd been through in her short life. She was such a little trouper.

The entrance foyer was only big enough to hold a shoe shelf and a rack of coat hooks. Tanja unlocked the door and backed into the corner as she opened it.

"Sorry, I thought it was op…" She trailed off as she saw it wasn't Shonda on her stoop.

Her heart went into free fall.

How many times had she waited and yearned and willed for this to happen? Leon. Here. As recently as yesterday afternoon, when she'd left her divorce certificate in the fireproof cabinet at the marina, she had spared a moment to wish for him to appear and tell her this wasn't what he wanted.

And she had told herself *again* to quit being a fool. He wasn't coming. He was never coming.

But here he was, tall and lean, casually perfect in faded jeans and a light windbreaker. Fine sparkles of raindrops sat on his hair like glitter. His mirrored aviators accentuated his trimmed beard and stern mouth.

Her heart commenced hammering. Her whole being took the hit of being in his presence again. She wanted to throw herself into his arms and say, *Yes, I'm still yours*.

But he had never wanted her, not really. Not the way she needed to be wanted.

She thought about closing the door on him, she really did, but she could never shut out someone she loved no matter how badly they'd hurt her.

"Come out of the rain." She stepped back so he could wipe his feet and follow her up the narrow staircase to the one-bedroom apartment over her brother's detached garage.

"This is nice," he said of the space with slanted ceilings, gabled windows, moss-green walls, and hardwood floors. The kitchen was galley style in a nook off the living area. It had a peninsula counter that jutted out to provide an eating area. It currently held her laptop and the job offers she'd been scrutinizing.

"Zach and Shonda were planning to rent it by the week to tourists, but they're letting me use it until I find a job and figure out what I can afford."

"You were supposed to use your settlement to buy

a house—" His breath sucked in as he caught sight of the crib tucked behind the pony wall at the top of the stairs.

He took off his sunglasses as he moved to look down on Illi. Her little arms were thrown up beside her curly hair, a corner of the knit blanket tangled in the fingers of one hand.

"She's growing," he said softly, moving her huggy bear into her side before he adjusted the blanket. His face spasmed with naked emotion as he looked down on her.

It was the most heartbreakingly beautiful thing Tanja had ever seen.

That's why he's here, she realized with a hard swallow. She wouldn't deny him time with Illi, either, even if it would cause her to feel jealous of her own daughter.

"Can I, um…" She had to clear her throat. "Can I make you some coffee?" She moved toward the kitchen.

"I miss you." He spoke so softly she was certain he was talking to the baby.

She turned to see it, to be included in some small way in his quiet admission to a sleeping baby. She told herself she only wanted to see him crack and reveal his love for her daughter, but he wasn't looking at Illi. He was looking at her.

The floor fell away and her entire being filled with helium. Not oxygen. No, there was not a bit of that in her right now.

"Both of you," he said with anguish creasing his

features. "I hate going home. It's not a home anymore. But I don't know how to ask you to come back and make it into one. I don't know what I could say that would convince you."

"You do," she said faintly. The buoyant hope inside her butted up against the shadows of despair she'd had to make into friends. "You just don't want to say it. And I understand why, but—"

"No, I do," he said with a rasp in his voice and a jerky step forward. His gaze went to the window where the white curtains glowed with a sudden burst of sunshine on this changeable spring day. "I think I've wanted to say it for a long time. Maybe I thought it wouldn't matter. That it wouldn't change anything because it never had in the past."

Tanja set down the ceramic mug she had drawn from the cupboard, afraid her numb fingers would drop it to smash at her feet.

"I think I would have said it five years ago if I'd had time to understand what this feeling is." He clenched his fist in front of his heart. "It hurts. You know? Like a muscle that aches so bad after a run you never want to exercise again. I'd almost rather throw up than feel this much. It's too intense to bear."

"It is," she said, biting her lip. "It was how I felt when you left me." Her lips trembled as she added, "And when I left you."

"I'm mad at you for that," he admitted with a ragged laugh. His clenched fist lowered. "Hypocritical, I know. I'm angry you divorced me even though it's what I said I wanted and you used the money in the best possible way. But I'm angry because I want to be your husband, Tanja. I want to be Illi's father and the father of as many kids as you want in whatever way you want to bring them into our lives. I love you. And I want you to love me, but—"

"No buts." She rushed toward him and he caught her so tightly she couldn't breathe, but she didn't care.

"Say it again," he commanded.

"I love you. That's all it is and all it has to be, Leon. I love you. So much."

He drew one shaken breath, then his mouth found hers. Their lips fused with perfection the way they always did, but with a new sweetness. The kiss was frantic with reunion, yet tender and familiar and new. It was imbued with a love that she was realizing had always been there, deep and soft and unacknowledged beneath every kiss they had ever exchanged.

Now it was real. True. Celebrated.

"Will you marry me?" He broke away only as far as he needed to whisper the proposal against her lips. "Again? This time I mean it. No escape clauses. We commit to facing our challenges together. Figure out how to get through them together because I will *never* let you go again."

She showed him her hand where his diamond band sat securely on her finger, teasing her with flashes of hope and memories of passion and the symbol of an everlasting love she would feel forever, whether he did or not.

He captured her hand and kissed the inside of her

wrist, clearly moved and not ashamed to let her see the sheen of emotion in his eyes. "You humble me."

"I don't think I could ever *not* feel married to you."

"Me, either," he said with bemusement. "I'm yours. I always will be."

Tanja had always had love in her life, but she had never known this kind. It filled her until she could hardly bear the breadth of it, but it was so good, she greedily let it grow bigger and bigger inside her.

They kissed and kissed, but it wasn't enough expression for the feelings that were surging between them, reacting and expanding. He lifted his head to glance toward the bedroom door. She drew him toward the tiny bedroom with its queen mattress in a wrought-iron frame. They sank onto the down-filled coverlet with mutual sighs.

The light shifted against the small window above the headboard, dimming. Rain began a homey patter against the roof as they tugged at each other's clothing, pressing kisses against each bit of skin they exposed.

"I want to spend all day touching and kissing and feeling you," he rasped. "I need every part of you." His heart was slamming so hard she felt it against her own. "But realistically...?" he asked ruefully.

"Thirty minutes," Tanja said on a soft laugh. "If we're lucky."

They got down to the serious business of reconciling. When he pressed inside her, their joining was deeply powerful, not simply because they'd been apart, but because their hearts were no longer shielded. Not one tiny bit.

"I love watching you come apart," he said as he moved within her, gaze tender as it was locked with hers. "I love knowing this is as good for you as it is for me."

"So good. Leon, I can't wait…" She speared her fingers into his hair and arched as climax gripped her.

He quickened his pace, taking her over the edge and tumbling with her into the joyous chasm of completion.

They cuddled under the blankets after, naked and glowing, caressing and murmuring lazily about how they might split their time between here and Greece.

"You would spend that much time here for me?" she asked. She'd seen his life in Greece. It was very demanding, not something he could drop on a whim.

"You are the breath in my sails," he said with a playful nibble of her chin. "I'll go wherever you take me. Isn't that obvious? Istuval. Parenthood…" He was teasing her, but that had been so poetic she teared up. *"Agape mou,"* he chided tenderly, kissing her better.

A questioning squawk of noise came from the other room. It was Illi's usual noise that announced she'd awakened and wished to be noticed.

Leon and Tanja exchanged a look. Tanja's chest swelled with anticipation as Leon fairly leaped from the bed to slip on his underwear. She pulled on his shirt and followed as far as the bedroom door, biting her lip.

"Louloudi mou," he greeted as he approached the crib, calling her "flower" in the endearingly tender

voice that undid everything inside Tanja. "How are you? I've missed you."

Illi let out a happy crow of excitement, one loud enough to cause ear damage, but it made them both laugh through their winces, especially because her little limbs went everywhere.

"I was afraid she'd forgotten me," he said with amused pleasure while Tanja clutched her heart and wondered how anyone could.

He cradled Illi into his shoulder and she curled herself into him, head on his shoulder while she bounced with delight.

Tanja was pretty sure her heart was going to bust right out of her chest.

Leon brought Illi to the bed and they played with her between them, exchanging light kisses over her excited squirms.

"Did I mention I want more kids?" He had hold of Illi's foot and was rubbing his closely trimmed beard against her sole. "Not right this second. I think we should at least get married again—"

"I'm sorry I divorced you," she said sheepishly.

"Don't do it again," he said lightly, but there was a flash of bleak pain in the dark depths of his eyes.

"Leon," she breathed with remorse, and reached for him.

"My fault." He caught her hand and kissed her palm. He might have left it there, but he met her gaze and admitted, "But I felt like you'd cut us apart. Like I'd lost you forever. It hurt like hell. I won't pretend it didn't. That's how I know I won't let it happen again."

He gently crushed her hand as though stamping the truth of his words into her skin and bones. "It didn't help one bit that I'd told you to do it. When I saw what you did with the money, though, I was glad you took it. Thank you for making that right." He kissed her fingertips, then his mouth twitched. "I saw your brother while I was there. He threatened to kill me," he said conversationally. "I pointed out that since you and Illi are my beneficiaries, that might look suspicious. I think we're good now."

"Leon, you didn't." She closed her eyes, never once having considered that she stood to inherit her husband's vast fortune.

"What? Who else am I going to leave it to? You're my *wife*. Do you want a big wedding this time?"

"No." She cupped his stubbled cheek. "I want you. Just you. That's all I've ever wanted."

"Same." He leaned across and they kissed. "You're all I will ever need. Well…" He sent a significant look to their daughter.

Tanja wrinkled her nose ruefully. "Same."

A week later, Leon bought a piece of property overlooking the ocean. When his mother and Cornelius arrived a few days after that, they all convened on the site of their future home. Leon and Tanja spoke their vows with their most cherished loved ones in attendance.

This time they meant it.

EPILOGUE

Five years later...

"BUT I'LL STILL live with you," Illi said anxiously, her legs tight around Leon's waist, her arm around his neck, her hand in his.

"You absolutely will," Leon told his daughter. "You will live with me forever." He briefly squished her tighter against him. "Even if you get married and have children and grandchildren. I love you too much to ever let you live with anyone else or go anywhere without me."

She giggled. "I have to go to school by myself. And you don't live with Yaya," she said, referring to his mother.

Smart as a whip, she was, and had a wonderful streak of independence he adored as much as every other part of her.

"How about this? You can always live with me if you want to. Will that work?"

"Yes." She nodded.

He kissed her forehead, not telling her he already resented having to share her with schoolteachers.

"Did it land?" Tanja asked as she returned with their son's hand clutched in her own.

"It did." He nodded at the flight board above where they stood.

Christo put his arms up, wanting Leon to hold him, too. He scooped up their toddler and asked him, "Did you go?"

Christo nodded.

"No. Just me," Tanja said ruefully. She was in the middle of carrying their next son or daughter, so a lot of Christo's potty training attempts were falling on her since she was always headed that direction anyway.

Leon loved seeing her pregnant, with her features round and sensual and rosy. Hell, he loved her when she was asleep or awake, sweaty from a workout or polished for an evening out. Grouchy from a bad night with a fussy baby or irreverently teasing him into laughter.

He loved her right now, trying to pretend she wasn't nervous as a mama duck and fierce as a mama bear beneath her glow of anticipation.

It had taken years to find Brahim and sort out his immigration. He wasn't a child any longer. He was nineteen and had wanted to come to Canada, even though things in Istuval had stabilized.

Leon had an office tower in Vancouver and Tanja would be off work with the new baby, so they had decided the city would become their base while Brahim settled in his new home. Illi was enrolled in a local school in the fall. They had a comfortable home on the north shore that would give Brahim an option between a guest house by the pool or a room inside the mansion with them.

First though, they would spend the summer at their home in Tofino, where the pace of life was slower and the rest of Tanja's family was looking forward to opening their arms and homes to their newest member.

"Thank you for this," Tanja said with a squeeze of Leon's arm when passengers began streaming from the secured area.

"Your children are my children. You know that."

She gave him a shaky, touched smile and a kiss, then turned to watch for Brahim.

Leon didn't have misgivings precisely, but he was fiercely protective of his family. Brahim had spent years as a drafted child soldier in a mercenary force. That sort of experience had to leave scars, so he was experiencing some apprehension even as he knew they would get through any bumps or nicks that might come about.

A few minutes later, a gasp was torn from Tanja's throat. She rushed toward a lanky young man, tall and dark wearing tattered jeans and an army green T-shirt.

He was looking up to read the unfamiliar signage and startled when Tanja was suddenly in front of him.

He was disoriented and surprised, but his reaction was immediate. He dropped his duffel and hugged Tanja with such tangible relief it cracked Leon's heart clean down the middle.

"Is that him?" Illi slid down from Leon's secure hold.

He watched her walk forward, faltering slightly when Brahim released Tanja to look at her belly. His smile was exactly like his sister's, full of happy wonder as he said something that made her laugh.

He looked searchingly past her and froze as he saw Illi.

Leon held his breath, protectiveness surging anew in him.

"Illi." Brahim covered his mouth and sank to one knee. His eyes grew bright, and he blinked them fast and hard. He held out a hand. "Look at you. Our mother would be so proud if she could see you," he said in a choked voice.

Without any urging, she rushed in for a hug.

He clutched her tight, eyes closed, yet he showed such gentleness that Leon's throat tightened.

Tanja came back to him and buried her face in Leon's shoulder, trembling and clearly overcome. Hell, he could hardly withstand the intensity of this reunion.

"Mama?" Christo touched her hair.

"I'm okay, little man. Mommy's just really, really happy." She showed him her beaming smile and round cheeks tracked with tears. "Your brother is here."

Christo looked at her belly, making her laugh and stammer out, "The other one."

Brahim was asking Illi questions. Illi was nodding and wiping at her little cheeks, smiling as she shyly answered. When Brahim rose and shouldered his duffel, Illi took his hand, drawing forth a very naked look of love as he gazed down on her.

Illi seemed to have an instant case of the hero worships. She brought him to Leon. "This is my daddy and my brother, Christo. This is my brother, Brahim."

"Leon. Welcome." Leon released Tanja to offer his hand.

Brahim shook it, but his expression shuttered slightly, telling Leon the young man's trust wouldn't be won as easily by him as it had been by Tanja and Illi.

Christo dipped out of Leon's hold straight into Brahim's arms, though. Brahim caught the boy with surprise.

"You give hugs, too?" Brahim asked in accented English. "Thank you." He patted Christo's back with bemusement, making them all laugh.

"Christo always wants to do everything I do," Illi informed in the very important tone of a big sister.

"Well, he is obviously learning to be as loving as you are." He gave Christo back to Leon, but his defensiveness had receded a little.

Hours later, when they had made the final leg of travel home and everyone was abed under one roof, Leon said, "I told Brahim he could talk to me about his experiences if he's worried it might burden you.

Or that we could find him a professional. He's liable to have PTSD or other lingering effects."

"Thank you for reaching out to him like that. I don't know that he's had any good male role models for a long time." She pinched his side, warning, "Don't say anything self-deprecating. You *are* a good role model."

"I'll defer to your better judgment," he said drily. "But I think we'll all be good for him." He cuddled his warm, supportive, incredibly generous wife into his side. "He's cautious, which is understandable, but the children will win him over. And you love so hard, you're impossible to resist."

"So do you. Is that news to you?"

He rolled and adjusted their positions so they were face-to-face. He smoothed a tendril of hair off her face.

"I didn't know I was capable of loving this much. I don't know that anyone else could have brought it out in me. And even though I don't know how all of this will work out, I know it will. That you and I will get through it, one way or another, together. Stronger."

"Leon." She cupped his jaw, and he drew her closer for a kiss.

She'd come to bed in a nightgown, already yawning, but desire sent his hands in search of skin. She made one of those receptive noises that turned him on, and they gravitated into each other.

"It's been a long day." He ran his mouth down her neck, inhaling her familiar scent. "I wasn't sure you'd want to."

"I always want to," she assured him, peeling her nightgown up. "I want *you*. I love you."

He set about demonstrating that his love and desire was as steadfast as hers.

* * * * *

Hooked by What the Greek's Wife Needs?
Dive into these other stories by Dani Collins!

Innocent in the Sheikh's Palace
Confessions of an Italian Marriage
Beauty and Her One-Night Baby
A Hidden Heir to Redeem Him

Available now!

#3885 AFTER THE BILLIONAIRE'S WEDDING VOWS...
by Lucy Monroe
Greek tycoon Andros's whirlwind romance with Polly started white-hot. Five years later, the walls he's built threaten to push her away forever! With his marriage on the line, Andros must win back his wife. Their passion still burns bright, but can it break down their barriers?

#3886 FORBIDDEN HAWAIIAN NIGHTS
Secrets of the Stowe Family
by Cathy Williams
Max Stowe is commanding and completely off-limits as Mia Kaiwi's temporary boss! But there's no escape from temptation working so closely together... Dare she explore their connection for a few scorching nights?

#3887 THE PLAYBOY PRINCE OF SCANDAL
The Acostas!
by Susan Stephens
Prince Cesar will never forgive polo star Sofia Acosta for the article branding him a playboy! But to avoid further scandal he must invite her to his lavish banquet in Rome. Where he's confronted by her unexpected apology and their *very* obvious electricity!

#3888 THE MAN SHE SHOULD HAVE MARRIED
by Louise Fuller
Famed movie director Farlan has come a long way from the penniless boy whose ring Nia rejected. But their surprise reunion proves there's one thing he'll never be able to relinquish...their dangerously electric connection!

"Mr. Alexandris," Tansy pronounced rather stiffly.

"Come sit down," he invited lazily. "Tea or coffee?"

"Coffee please," Tansy said, following him around a sectional room divider into a rather more intimate space furnished with sumptuous sofas and then sinking down into the comfortable depths of one, her tense spine rigorously protesting that amount of relaxation.

She was fighting to get a grip on her composure again but nothing about Jude Alexandris in the flesh matched the formal online images she had viewed. He wasn't wearing a sharply cut business suit—he was wearing faded, ripped and worn jeans that outlined long, powerful thighs and narrow hips and accentuated the prowling natural grace of his every movement. An equally casual dark gray cotton top complemented the jeans. One sleeve was partially pushed up to reveal a strong brown forearm and a small tattoo that appeared to be printed letters of some sort. His garb reminded her that although he might be older than her, he was still only in his late twenties, and that unlike her, he had felt no need to dress to impress.

Her pride stung at the knowledge that she was little more than a commodity on Alexandris's terms. Either he would choose her or he wouldn't. She had put herself on the market to be bought, though, she thought with sudden self-loathing. How could she blame Jude Alexandris for her stepfather's use of virtual blackmail to get her agreement? Everything she was doing was for Posy, she reminded herself squarely, and the end would justify the means...wouldn't it?

"So..." Tansy remarked in a stilted tone because she was determined not to sit there acting like the powerless person she knew herself to be in his presence. "You require a fake wife..."

HPEXP0121

Jude shifted a broad shoulder in a very slight shrug. "Only we would know it was fake. It would have to seem real to everyone else from the start to the very end," he advanced calmly. "Everything between us would have to remain confidential."

"I'm not a gossip, Mr. Alexandris." In fact, Tansy almost laughed at the idea of even having anyone close enough to confide in, because she had left her friends behind at university, and certainly none of them had seemed to understand her decision to make herself responsible for her baby sister rather than return to the freedom of student life.

"I trust no one," Jude countered without apology. "You would be legally required to sign a nondisclosure agreement before I married you."

"Understood. My stepfather explained that to me," Tansy acknowledged, her attention reluctantly drawn to his careless sprawl on the sofa opposite, the long, muscular line of a masculine thigh straining against well-washed denim. Her head tipped back, her color rising as she made herself look at his face instead, encountering glittering dark eyes that made the breath hitch in her throat.

"I find you attractive, too," Jude Alexandris murmured as though she had spoken.

"I don't know what you're talking about," Tansy protested, the faint pink in her cheeks heating exponentially. Her stomach flipped while she wondered if she truly could be read that easily by a man.

"For this to work, we would need that physical attraction. Nobody is likely to be fooled by two strangers pretending what they don't feel, least of all my family, some of whom are shrewd judges of character."

Tansy had paled. "Why would we need attraction? I assumed this was to be a marriage on paper, nothing more."

"Then you assumed wrong," Jude told her without skipping a beat.

Don't miss
The Greek's Convenient Cinderella
available February 2021 wherever
Harlequin Presents books and ebooks are sold.

Harlequin.com

Love Harlequin romance?

DISCOVER.

Be the first to find out about promotions, news and exclusive content!

 Facebook.com/HarlequinBooks

 Twitter.com/HarlequinBooks

Instagram.com/HarlequinBooks

Pinterest.com/HarlequinBooks

ReaderService.com

EXPLORE.

Sign up for the Harlequin e-newsletter and download a free book from any series at **TryHarlequin.com**

CONNECT.

Join our Harlequin community to share your thoughts and connect with other romance readers! **Facebook.com/groups/HarlequinConnection**